Hoofprints on the Moon

For Shasta

Patricia Duncan

Hoofprints on the Moon

Patricia Duncan

Press, LLC

© 2015 Patricia Duncan. All Rights Reserved.

No part of this book may be used or reproduced or transmitted in any form or by any means, electronic or mechanical, including photocopying, recording, or by any information storage or retrieval system without written permission except in the case of brief quotations used in critical articles and reviews. Request for permissions should be addressed to the publisher:

Good Oak Press, LLC
P.O. Box 12195
Tucson, Arizona 85732

Editor: Cynthia Roedig
Cover Design: Good Oak Press, LLC
Cover Illustration: Wes Lowe
Typesetting: Good Oak Press, LLC

Printed in the United States of America

ISBN : 978-0991089352

This book is a work of fiction. The characters in this story are fictitious. Any and all real locations have been used fictitiously and without any intent to describe any real individuals who may be affiliated with those locations. Any resemblance to any actual persons, living or dead, is purely coincidental.

To all young people who dream of horses

PART 1
CHAPTER ONE

Kentucky 1950

A prickly sensation ran up Amanda's spine. She couldn't ever remember seeing this strange, yellow light blurring the white-fenced pastures. A smell of dampness hung in the air. The leaves on the oak trees were limp and still. Even the birds had stopped singing.

She paced the kitchen floor. Her cotton shirt stuck to her back. She stopped and looked at her watch for the tenth time in as many minutes. Pushing the screen door open, she stood on the wide veranda, looking to the west. Lightning slashed across purple clouds, a second later thunder rolled over the hills. "It's coming closer," she said under her breath.

Her parents, Kathy and Jim McKenzie, had left her in charge of the stables this afternoon and of their fifteen thoroughbred horses while they attended an auction in nearby Westchester. This was the first time in the twelve years of her life that she'd been responsible for the place most of the day.

I want everything to go perfectly. I want my folks to know I'm growing up and they can depend on me. She stood looking across the rolling hills. "There is something scary about today," she whispered.

She had looked at this scene since the first time she could toddle to the door and peek out. She had never seen it look the way it looked this afternoon. It wasn't quite five o'clock, yet luminous, amber light was blurring the shapes of massive oak trees, the sloping green lawns and distant whitewashed stables. *I think I'll feed a little early tonight.*

Amanda ran down the stone steps and to the long horse barn. There's nothing to worry about, she told herself, hoping it was true. She slid the barn door open, slipped through and pulled it shut. She leaned against the door for a moment, feeling her heart pounding against her ribs. The spotless stable felt cool. Sounds of horses rummaging in their hay and the sweet smell of alfalfa helped her stop trembling. The first raindrops thudded on the metal roof.

Amanda looked down the long rows of Dutch doors, most of them with the top half thrown open. A few horses had their heads out, nickering to her. Summer Star's stall was the third one on the left. It was still three weeks until the mare was due to give birth, but tonight the girl did not hear the usual welcoming whinny and the white-blazed face of her mare was not shining over the stall door. She raced to the empty opening.

The horse stood in the center of the box stall, front legs splayed apart and nostrils flared. A spasm shook the mare's body. When it passed, she snorted, threw her head high and began to pace. *Star's in labor. The foal is coming.* Her father had told her exactly what to do if this should happen. Dan, the veterinarian, is just a phone call away.

The rain drummed louder now and wind gusts moaned through the building's hayloft, swinging the rusted hay arm with a repeated creak and clank. Amanda unlatched the stall door and rushed in. She ran her hand along the back of the heavily breathing animal, clucking softly.

"I'll be right back, Star," she whispered into one ear. Ducking under the rope across the stall door, she ran to the opposite end of the barn, pushed the tack room door open, ran to the phone on the wall and dialed. On the third ring she heard the Vet's familiar voice.

"Dan, its Amanda McKenzie. Star's in labor and I'm here alone. Mom and Dad are at the auction." She was surprised to hear her voice sound higher than usual.

"Okay, Amanda, I'm on my way." A brilliant flash of light filled the small room and thunder hit with a jolt that shook the plank floor. "Just a little storm passing through, Honey. You go keep Star focused on her job and I'll be there in a jiffy."

Before she could answer, a bolt of lightning turned the room blue-white and the frame building shook. Then complete silence. The phone line was dead. She stood holding the receiver, rooted in place for a moment.

The sound of hailstones on the metal roof startled her into action. She ran through the doorway and down the wide aisle. A horse's muzzle reached out from each doorway. The animals looked skittish, stretching their necks toward the girl, whinnying, pawing the earth or nervously shaking their heads. "There's nothing to be afraid of, just a little storm passing through." Unconsciously she repeated Dan's words. She slowed to rub a nose, pat a neck or smooth a forelock. *I can't let the horses know I'm scared*, she thought. Flashes of lightning continued to bathe the barn in light, thunder shook and hail began to batter like a thousand exploding shells. The noise shut out everything else.

* * *

When Amanda called, Dan had answered in his office, so his bag was on the table. *This weather looks foul. Better get started.* He clicked the black satchel open to be sure he had everything he'd need in case the birth was complicated, shrugged into his jacket, checked his pockets for the keys to his old pick-up and was on his way. He turned his rig south on the blacktop, ground the gears into third and headed toward McKenzie's.

The sky was tarnished pewter, sliced open with daggers of lightning. The thunder was deafening. Then he saw it. Outlined against the dark sky was an even darker funnel shape, moving from his left to right, a mile or two in the distance. It suddenly veered toward the pickup. Dan braked and threw himself to the floor of the cab.

The truck was lifted into the air like a match box toy, spun around and then, miraculously, set back on the ground.

The world was as soundless as a tomb. Dan slowly raised his head, then pulled himself off the floorboards and crawled onto the seat. He peered out. The scene around him, dimly lit and eerily quiet, looked like an artist's painting of Hades. Uprooted trees were crisscrossed, the fingers of their roots forming spidery shapes against the sky. The rain pounded down and the smell of damp earth filled the air.

Cautiously the vet opened the cab door and dropped to the ground. Taking a deep breath, he steadied himself against the cab. "No point in trying to drive," he muttered. "Better see if I can find the road under all this mess." He reached into the cab, picked up his bag, jacket and emergency flashlight. It was going to be a long walk.

* * *

Amanda ducked into Star's stall. The mare moved toward her with frightened eyes rolled wide, showing white at the edges. "There's nothing to be afraid of," the girl whispered. "Dan will be here soon." She put her arms around her mare's neck. "You and I can handle this 'til he comes. We're a team, remember?" She checked the water, dragged a bale of hay into the stall and spread it around. She continued to talk softly to the mare.

When Amanda turned her full attention back to her horse, she gasped. Star stood with her head lowered, long, slender legs braced apart, breathing deeply. Sweat glistened on her distended sides and she seemed to be listening to an inner voice. *"It's going so fast,"* Amanda thought. *"Hurry, Dan."*

From the other stalls, she heard kicks splintering wood, snorts and frightened whinnies. Amanda wound one hand through Star's forelock and threw the other arm around her neck. She pressed her head close to the mare's cheek, "I've got to leave you for a minute. The other horses are spooked. I'll be back as fast as I can. Don't be scared. Dan's coming." She didn't notice that each time she spoke, the unborn foal reacted. The mare's side was jolted from within by the kick of a tiny hoof.

The girl crouched under the rope and quickly began the rounds, trying to reassure one animal after another. She fed each one a flake of hay and closed their doors top and bottom. At the end of the barn, the sliding door was still open. Pulling it closed, she saw it—looming against the dark sky was a darker grey funnel roaring across the countryside. Tornado!

She rushed back to her mare. The horse lay on the hay, bathed in sweat, breathing in quick gasps. "Help me to know what to do." Amanda didn't realize she spoke aloud. Again, the sound of her voice brought sharp movements from the unborn baby. She wiped damp strands of hair from her forehead with trembling hands, turned to Summer Star and took a deep breath.

She began to talk to her mare, saying anything that came into her mind, keeping the sound of her voice as steady as she could. She had watched two other births and she remembered what she had seen her Dad do. Her throat felt dry.

She saw two tiny hooves emerging from the birth canal. Kneeling, she grasped the little pasterns and applied gentle pressure. Slowly the forelegs became visible, followed by the head tucked between them, next the shoulders and then, almost before she knew it, the perfectly formed colt lay in the hay beside her.

Amanda felt warm tears on her cheeks. She picked up two handfuls of hay and began to rub and massage the small, wet body, drying him. The foal tried to brace his long front legs against the floor. First one and then the other collapsed at the knee and he sprawled on the hay.

Amanda sat propped against the side wall of the stall, smiling. She didn't know how tired she was until this minute. Star seemed pretty well spent, too, but raised her head, grunted and struggled to her feet. She shook herself and blew through her nostrils to clear the hay dust. Her first born staggered to his feet. For a long moment he stood unsteadily and looked at Amanda before he wobbled to his mother.

The storm faded into the distance. Thunder murmured far away, the rain now only a whisper on the roof, the wind a sigh. Peaceful sounds drifted to Amanda from the nearest stalls; horses moving quietly in their familiar surroundings, pulling at their manger hay, blowing lazily. She lay down on the sweet smelling bed and watched the two beautiful animals. Soon the foal dropped awkwardly to the ground. Before he tucked his head between his knees, he turned large, dark eyes toward Amanda and held hers, locked in his steady gaze. Amanda could not look away. She stared into those eyes and knew in her heart he had been a part of her always.

* * *

A tired Dan reached the McKenzie's driveway just as Amanda's parents pulled in from the opposite direction and jumped from their car. When they saw Dan, they ran to him. "What on earth happened to you?" they called in unison.

Dan held up a hand "I drove into a tornado." This was met with a gasp. "It went south of here; looks like your place wasn't touched. I was on my way here, because Amanda called and said Star was in labor."

Amanda's mother, Kathy, put her hand to her mouth, "Oh, she must have been so frightened."

They turned and ran down the sloping lawn to the stables, pulled the heavy door open and rushed along the central corridor to Star's stall, where they found Amanda asleep in the hay, her mare dozing beside her and the newborn colt stretched out between them.

CHAPTER TWO

The next morning Garth, Amanda's lifelong friend and classmate, was lying in bed putting off getting up. He heard the jangle of the phone, threw back the covers and ran down stairs, catching it on the third ring.

"Hi, Garth, it's me. Did I get you out of bed?"

"Hi, Amanda. I was awake, just being lazy."

"Star had her foal last night. I was here alone and helped Star deliver him." She sounded excited. "We're going to name him Tornado 'cause of the storm. Can you come over?"

"I'm on my way." He charged up the stairs two at a time, showered and was ready in fifteen minutes. It was Saturday and the old, Georgian house was quiet. He opened his little brother's door and peered into the darkened room. Still asleep. Pete was going to be disappointed when he found out Garth had seen the foal without him.

Easing the door closed, he went back to the kitchen, swung his long leg over a chair, poured milk on corn flakes and wolfed them down. Grabbing three doughnuts from the counter, he shoved two in his pockets, held one in his mouth and wrote a quick note to his mom, adding a PS, "Tell Pete I'll take him to see the colt this afternoon." Twenty minutes from the time he hung up he was on his bike, pedaling down the valley.

He looked at his watch, leaned over the handle bars and decided to see if he could break his old record. McKenzie's place was about three miles south of his family's spread. He'd ridden this stretch so many times he no longer saw the rolling hills of blue grass or the whitewashed fences and elm trees forming a canopy over the road.

He pumped the last quarter mile with legs driving like pistons. There she was, sitting on the porch steps. He threw one fist up in the air as he skidded up to her. "Ten minutes. That's the best yet."

She jumped up laughing, grabbed his hand and led him to the barns. They slowed near the door of Star's stall. She called her mare's name and they peeked in.

"White," Garth cried. "Thoroughbred's are never born white, unless…"

"No, he's not an albino. See his dark eyes."

"That's the biggest, newborn foal I ever saw."

"Dad and Dan think he'll be over eighteen hands."

Garth and Amanda spoke the same language: his parents also owned a large horse-breeding farm and raised horses to compete in the show jumping arena.

The colt tottered to the door and raised his tiny nose to touch the girl's fingers. She turned and looked eagerly at Garth, waiting for his reaction.

"Amanda, I think he's the most beautiful colt I've ever seen." For once, Garth wasn't teasing.

CHAPTER THREE

Three Years Later

The morning began for Amanda like any other. She hummed to herself as she crossed the lawn from her house to the stables. She wore tan britches and low-topped, jodhpur boots. Her dark hair was pulled back in a blue ribbon.

When she was about twenty yards from the barn, she stopped and began to tiptoe. Before she reached the corner, she heard a shrill whinny. Peeping around the building, she saw the gleaming white head of her stallion stretched over the stall door toward her. "Darn it, why can't I ever sneak up on you?" she asked him.

While she brushed his silken coat, she held her usual conversation with him. "Someday you're going to be famous, you know." The stallion watched her with attentive eyes. "You're going to be the World Champion High Jumper." Tornado's ears twitched forward and back.

Amanda continued to talk to him while she saddled and bridled her horse. "How long are you going to keep growing?" She dragged a stool over beside him.

You're already the biggest horse in the stable." Stepping up on the stool, she put her left foot in the stirrup and swung into the flat English saddle.

It was April and the morning held the promise of summer. "Can you guess where we're heading?" she asked him as they trotted up the tree-lined drive. "Yep, we're going to meet Garth. Did I ever tell you how much I like him?" She laughed, "Only about a million times, huh?"

A red cardinal darted from a low branch and swooped across the road in front of them. Tornado snorted and pranced sideways in mock fear. "Feel like showing off a bit?" He swished his tail and tossed his long silver mane.

Amanda spotted Garth before he saw her. She could see his tousled thatch of blond hair flickering through the sunlit patches. She pulled up a minute and watched him riding through the trees on his chestnut mare. No wonder all the girls swoon over him, she thought.

Garth caught sight of her, clucked his mare, Annie, into a trot and jogged up beside her, open-mouthed in pretend amazement. "What a surprise meeting you here." He grinned his lop-sided grin. "Tornado looks full of it this morning."

"I've been telling him he's going to be a champion some day. I think it went to his head."

Turning the horses, they rode through the familiar bluegrass valleys. They glanced up as they passed the iron gates of the Duke estate, where Buddy and Millicent lived with their father, Laurence Duke. He had arrived in the valley eleven years earlier, purchased a large tract of land and built a sprawling, Tudor mansion for himself and his two children. There was much speculation among his neighbors about where he had come from and where he had made his fortune. It remained a mystery.

"Something about that place gives me the willies," Amanda said.

"Yeah, it's kinda grim looking. I 'spose that proves something about having too much money. I wouldn't mind trying for a while, though." They both laughed and rode on.

"Your friend, Paul, called me this morning," Amanda told him.

Garth looked at her. His crooked grin faded. "What'd he want?"

Amanda shrugged. "To say hello, I guess."

Garth grunted.

Is he jealous of Paul? She wondered. The corners of her mouth crept up. Before she could savor that thought, Garth's mare squealed and leaped four-footed off the ground, then whirled and raced back down the path as he struggled to pick up the reins. He and the horse thundered around the bend and out of sight.

Tornado froze. His front legs were stiff and planted wide apart. The girl stood in the stirrups, craning to see what had startled the horses.

That's when it happened.

Her mind exploded into another dimension. She had felt this before with Tornado, but never with the force that hit her today. She could see nothing around her. She felt the hairs on her arms prickle with goose bumps. The eerie image of a coiled rattlesnake, head and tail rattles raised, burst into her darkened mind. It felt like sitting in a movie theater with nothing on the screen but wall-to-wall snake. She couldn't see the trees around her, couldn't see the path, the grass, the sky. She could only see the coiled snake.

In a few seconds, the vision passed. Tornado snorted and backed, tucking his hind quarters under, front legs like ramrods. He arched his neck; he zeroed in on an area twenty feet ahead and to the right. Then she heard the ominous sound of rattles. She pulled up the reins and urged the stallion farther back, just as Garth and the mare reappeared.

Amanda fought to get her breath. It had never been this bad.

* * *

When Annie took off with Garth, the two of them shot down the trail for a couple of a hundred feet while he struggled to control the terrified horse. He managed to pull her to a halt. "What got into you, lady?" He patted her neck and talked to her. "Something pretty scary, huh? Let's go check it out."

After some coaxing, he turned her back to the spot where he'd left Amanda. When they rounded the corner, he saw the girl sitting stiff and motionless on her big, white stallion. "Don't know what spooked Annie," he called. "I thought she was on her way to Springdale." He stopped when he saw Amanda's face.

"A snake..." her voice broke. "A rattler."

"Did you see it?" *What's wrong with her*, he thought. "Are you OK?"

She nodded.

"Where is it?"

She pointed with a trembling finger. "In that clearing across from the big Hickory."

He dismounted, handed Amanda his reins, picked up a heavy rock and started gingerly in that direction. "Got it," he yelled a minute later. When Garth got back to Amanda, he saw her try to smile. He studied her face. Is it really the snake she is so afraid of?

They turned and headed home. Amanda did not speak. He took her hint and the two rode a while in silence.

At last Amanda took a breath and said, "Garth, do you remember the day we took Peter and Tornado with us on a picnic and how easily Tornado kept finding Pete?"

* * *

Peter, Garth's brother, had been just nine years old at the time. Amanda, Garth, Pete and Tornado were playing tag and hide and seek. Amanda told Garth she wanted to try an experiment. She sensed something between Tornado and herself—something that scared her a little. The colt always seemed to know when she was near, he listened to her when she spoke and kept his eyes on her and his attention focused. He knew what she wanted before she asked.

During the next game, Garth saw her watch Peter run up a small hill and crouch behind a tree. She looked at Tornado and the horse stopped, turned to Amanda, then spun toward the oak and galloped to the top of the knoll.

"You got me," Peter shouted from the top of the hill. "How the heck do you do that?"

Garth came out of his hiding place. "What's going on, Amanda? How does he do that?"

* * *

Amanda went on, "Just now was like that time, only more so. It happened when your horse took off. I saw a coiled rattler, but not with my eyes. I saw it in my head. I couldn't see anything around me, just this big picture of a snake. I think…"

Garth turned in his saddle and looked at her. "You never really saw the snake?" She shook her head. "Do you think Tornado did?" Amanda looked away and nodded. Garth shaded his eyes with his hand, watching her.

"I feel like I should dust off my broomstick," Amanda said with a nervous laugh.

"Do you believe in mental telepathy or ESP or that kinda stuff?"

"I do now," she answered. "Do you think I'm… weird?"

"Gosh, no. I think it's neat."

She sighed. "It's a creepy feeling." The little worry line on her forehead softened. They didn't talk about it again, but neither of them forgot.

CHAPTER FOUR

One afternoon Amanda's father, Jim, sat beside his bay mare, wrapping the horse's sprained leg. A small man, with a tweed cap cocked over his eye, popped his head above the stall door, "Mornin' Guv'nor."

Jim started and turned his head. "Mornin' to you. What can I do for you?"

"Thought ye might be needin' some help 'round here," he said with a heavy Irish brogue. "I been workin' up to the Duke place as a groom, but they's a bit uppity fer the likes a me."

"Let me finish here and we'll talk about it." Jim turned back to his patient and fastened the bandage, wiped his hands on a towel and opened the stall door.

The little man jumped forward to hold it for him.

Amanda's father held out his hand. "The name's Jim McKenzie."

The stranger pulled his cap off and extended his hand. "Fitzgerald's me moniker. Fitz I'm called. Real pleased t'meetcha."

"Tell me about yourself."

"Well, Sir, I bin a jockey in me younger days. Rode at Bell Gardens and Saramac and all them big 'uns. Good I was, too, 'till one day I broke me hip in a bad pile up. Ain't been able t'ride much since. Gi' me a chance,

Guv'nor, and I'll work fer room and board and a bit extra fer sum spendin' money. I'm a real hard worker, real hard, ye'll see."

"You've come at a good time, Fitz. We've got more to do around here than we can handle. Tell you what, I'll give you a try for a week."

"Thankin' ye I be, Sir," Fitz said, replacing his worn cap. "If ye'll show me where t'put me things, I'll be getting right t'work. Ye'll not regret it, Sir."

CHAPTER FIVE

Across the valley at the Duke estate, Buddy Duke hopped out of bed at seven a.m. He showered and spent several minutes choosing the right shirt and pants for the day. He carefully parted his pale wisp of hair, smoothed the bedspread once more, straightened the towels in his bathroom, and went into the hall. He walked quietly to Millicent's bedroom door and listened.

"Is that you creeping around out there, Buddy?"

"Can I come in?"

"Door's open." His sister sat up with her black and white cat on her lap. A brown and white saddle shoe lay upside down in the middle of the carpet, the other poked from beneath the satin bedspread. A plaid skirt draped over the chair, a white blouse hung from the floor lamp and a cashmere cardigan was crumpled on the inlaid parquet. Powder dusted the dressing table where two lipsticks stood open with red columns twisted up, a hairbrush balanced half in and half out of the drawer. The bathroom door opened to a tangle of towels on the floor and a spilled bottle of vitamins.

"Geez, what a mess."

"That's what the maids are for, Bud."

"You look smug—thinking about Garth?"

"As a matter of fact, I was"

Buddy glanced around for a place to sit, and finally took the skirt off the chair and walked toward the closet. "Wish I had a chance with Amanda."

"Bud, just drop it on the floor, don't be such a fuss budget." He folded it in half and laid it across the window seat.

"Do you think she'd ever pay any attention to me? She's always with Garth."

Millicent looked him up and down. "Probably not." Buddy's face flushed. "Face it, Bud, Garth's a real dream boat. You aren't."

"I guess."

"I'm going to take Garth away from Amanda. That might help you. Saturday we'll all be at the Louisville Horse Show. Watch me turn this into an interesting weekend." She threw the cat off the bed. "Now get out of here so I can get dressed."

* * *

Garth loaded tack into their six-horse van. Pete struggled across the gravel with his English jumping saddle over his left arm, clutching its pommel in his right hand. He had been rubbing saddle soap into the leather for the last half hour. "Just get my bridle and I'm ready." His voice sounded tight.

"Nervous, pal?"

"Some. Did you do well in your first big show?"

"Think I got fifth."

"Hope I can ride like you someday."

Garth reached out and rumpled his brother's hair. "You're going to do great tonight." Peter held up crossed fingers. "Go tell the folks we're ready."

Peter stowed his saddle with the rest of the tack in the van and headed for the house. Garth climbed into the back of the rig, pulled the ramp in behind him, bolted the door and sat on the hay, looking at six horse's heads. Idly, he rubbed the muzzle of the bay on his right. A furrow ran between his brows. Something had happened yesterday that still bugged him.

He'd been riding his bike when a big, black Cadillac pulled up beside him. The driver rolled down his darkened window and asked for directions to the Duke house. Garth caught a quick glimpse of four men wearing dark glasses. He thought he saw a shoulder holster. They reminded him of a Humphrey Bogart movie about Las Vegas gangsters. The car had Nevada plates. Why would these guys be looking for the Duke place?

His mind wandered to another problem. Paul hangs around Amanda all the time. She must like him or she'd tell him to get lost. His grey eyes cooled. Maybe I should give Amanda a taste of how I feel when I see her with Paul. Seeing more of Millicent will give me a chance to snoop around the Duke place at the same time. He gave the gelding's nose a final pat.

* * *

The brick stable at the Duke mansion was roofed in copper, like the house. The building had taken on a patina of age; the copper had turned greenish and ivy climbed over the bricks. A weather vane, topped with a rearing horse, turned lazily in the breeze.

A maroon and pale-grey horse van backed out of the garage and drove onto the concrete saddling area. Millicent Duke planted herself in the driveway and supervised the loading of the horses. The family's private trainer, Russell Long, looked on frowning. This was supposed to be his job.

Millicent wore tan britches and a checked, rat-catcher shirt, open at the neck. She had tied her thick, dark hair off her face in a pale ribbon. She held a riding crop in her right hand, slapping it against her leg when something displeased her, which was often. A young man with an acne-blotched face led a bay mare up the ramp.

"Bobby, watch what you're doing! Keep her in the middle of the ramp. If she slips she could break a leg."

Bobby shot her a look of loathing, but moved the mare over.

The girl continued to slap the crop against her boot. Bobby approached again, leading the grey gelding Millicent planned to ride in the hunter class.

"Give him to me." She pulled the lead rope from Bobby's hands, jerked it smartly and barked, "Pay attention." The animal flinched, but put his ears forward, kept his eye on the narrow, wooden planks and walked into the van. Millicent jumped down, looking pleased.

Bobby and the trainer raised the sloping, wooden walk, slammed the van door closed and slid the lock into place. "See you in Louisville." Russell touched his cap, walked around the van and climbed in the driver's seat. Bobby jumped up to the passenger side and the van moved up the driveway, slowed at the gates, turned south and was gone.

Millicent turned toward the house, where she spotted Buddy's pale face, quickly withdrawn from an upstairs window. She marched through the front door and found her father in his office, cradling the phone between shoulder and chin. He glanced up and motioned her to a chair. She tapped her foot impatiently, not listening to the conversation.

"Check the odds when it closes tonight." Her father puffed on a slender cigar. "I'll call you back in a minute." He clicked the phone down and looked up at his daughter.

"I see you're taking Spumoni and Black Diamond for Russell to ride," she said. "When do I ride in the "A" classes? I'm as good as he is."

"You think so?" Her father held the cheroot between his teeth, grinning. "I think I'll just call your bluff. You ride Diamond tonight."

"You've got a deal!" Millicent slapped the desk with her palm. She couldn't wait to see Garth's face when she appeared in the top flight "A" class. So far her plans were proceeding nicely.

Laurence Duke watched his daughter pace out of the room, then picked up the phone and spun the dial. He resumed his conversation, "Frankie, I've got another job for you." He leaned over the desk and pushed the door closed. "Yeah, the one we talked about." He listened a moment, sending plumes of cigar smoke circling. "I don't think he'd try that. If he does, you know what to do."

CHAPTER SIX

The afternoon breeze picked up, blowing in dark clouds. Amanda leaned forward in the green and white van with her chin resting on the back of the front seat. Her dad, Jim McKenzie, turned between brick pillars at the entrance to the Louisville show grounds and eased into the stable area, Kathy, her mother, beside him. Their hired man, Fitz, rode in the back with the horses. This was to be Tornado's first show.

Amanda could see Bannock's black and tan rig parked in front of the barn to the left. All around her blazed the colors of brightly painted horse vans, fluttering banners, exhibitors clad in red jackets, white britches and shining black boots. Horses wrapped in blue, green, red and purple blankets sashayed at the end of their lead ropes, grooms struggling to control them. The air rang with the shouts of handlers and the whinnying and snorting of the animals. Deep voiced announcements, which no one could understand, boomed from the loudspeaker.

"We're over there somewhere." Kathy pointed.

Jim maneuvered toward the barn, rolling down his window to call to Phil Bannock, "Hi, neighbor. Which side are we on?"

Garth's dad waved and Peter darted out of a stall and motioned the way, pointing to five box stalls marked McKenzie. Pete threw open the first stall door, bowing low and waving his right hand toward the opening.

Amanda jumped from the cab, opened the side door of the van and Fitz lowered the ramp. She ran up the ramp and led her stallion down the wooden incline and into the nearest box stall where Peter still held the door open. "How're you doing, Peter?" Amanda asked.

"OK, I guess."

"First show's a little scary, isn't it? First show for Tornado, too."

Peter nodded.

"You'll do great." She looked around, "Where's Garth?"

"Over at the arena somewhere."

Amanda turned to Tornado, resting her hand on the horse's shoulder. She felt him tremble and began to talk to him, running her hand over the stallion's silvery coat. Peter hung around, fidgeting, trying to be of help but squirming with impatience and chattering continually. Amanda glanced at him and smiled, "Let's walk the course, Pete.

"Yeah, I've got to plan my strategy."

The two wove their way between the polished trailers and dodged past horses wearing braids in their manes. They went through the tunnel marked "Entrants only." It took a moment for their eyes to adjust when they came out into the arena where the jumps were set up. Amanda breathed the fresh, forest smell of tanbark. She started to tingle. She turned to Peter, "Exciting, isn't it?"

"Makes my stomach feel kinda funny."

The course layouts were posted at the entrance gate. Peter found his class and traced the course with his finger, then jogged into the ring to inspect each jump. Amanda stepped forward and looked for the listing of her class.

"Hi, Amanda." Paul Norman and Craig Sutherland, school friends who also showed horses, came toward her from the opposite side of the arena. Amanda knew Garth was jealous of Paul and looked around for him. Paul walked with his usual swagger. His nose had been broken when a horse he rode threw his head up and smacked him in the face. The crooked tilt gave him a mischievous look and his brown eyes always seemed to be ready to laugh. Craig was a little taller and heavier than Paul, but seemed to fade into the background when the two were together.

"Did you bring your stallion?" Paul called as they neared.

"He's in the third class tonight."

"I'm glad I'm not entered in that one—I'd probably get beat. I hear he's really something."

"I'm so excited." Impulsively, Amanda took his hand and squeezed it. "But I'm scared, too." Then she heard Garth's deep voice. He and Millicent walked across the tanbark with Peter in tow. Amanda pulled her hand away from Paul's, but not before Garth saw it. She felt the blood rush to her face.

Millicent said something to Garth and he looked down at her and laughed. He doesn't have to laugh so hard, Amanda thought. She watched Millicent link her arm through Garth's and felt an odd little twist in her chest.

"I'm riding in the A class tonight," Millicent boasted. "Where are the A postings?"

Garth grinned, looking over his shoulder at Amanda. The pinch in her chest tightened.

Peter finished his ride triumphantly, cantering back to the barns with an ear-to-ear grin and a pink ribbon fluttering from his mare's headband. He pulled his horse's saddle and bridle off and threw a blanket over him. "I'll be back in a sec to take care of you," he promised and hurried to the ring to watch as much of the third class as he could.

While she saddled Tornado, Amanda explained to the young stallion what lay ahead for him in his first show appearance. "I know you've never been away from home." He swung his neck around and touched her left arm with his muzzle. Amanda closed the stall doors, took his head between her hands and whispered into his ear, "There'll be more people than you've ever seen and more noise than you've ever heard." She stroked his forelock and put her arms around his neck. "Don't be nervous. I'll be with you every minute." She gave him a last hug, and then slipped into her black hunt coat and the two headed to the arena.

Instead of speaking, she focused her mind on reassuring the horse about the moving sea of people around him, about the countless new smells and new sounds. He shied at a cat, and then sidestepped around a blue tack trunk, arching his neck and turning his head to keep an eye on it as they passed. They arrived at the gate as it swung open and the loudspeaker announced, "Now we have Tornado, a three-year-old from the McKenzie stable, making his first appearance in any show ring."

Amanda felt the power of her stallion beneath her as Tornado trotted into the arena. They galloped to the first rail jump and soared over. They turned to the center of the ring and took the in-and-out, striding just once between fences. *I'm actually starting to have fun*, she thought. The next jump stood four feet high, painted to resemble a stone wall. A little boy in the stands let go of his helium filled balloon just as Tornado approached. It bobbed across the horse's path and Amanda felt his body tense. *It's only a balloon, Tornado.* A long, purple ribbon dangled from the balloon and danced across the horse's line of vision. He snorted and took a prancing step sideways. *That's just a silly string tied to the balloon*, she reassured him with her thoughts.

The stallion turned his focus back to the jump ahead, clearing the barrier with half a foot to spare. Applause began. "Please stay quiet while these green horses are in the ring," the announcer cautioned. Tornado seemed to take wing over two brush jumps, a triple rail and zigzag. He slowed, circled and walked from the ring. The grandstand came alive with whistles and applause.

Jim and Fitz waited at the gate. Jim let out a triumphant whoop. "What an incredible performance. Even that darned balloon didn't bother him. This horse is sensational. I'm almost afraid to think what he might be able to do."

Amanda dropped the reins and threw her arms around her stallion's neck. "I knew you could do it," she sang to him. "I knew you could do it."

The rest of the evening her friends came to Tornado's stall to congratulate them. Garth came with a group, said "You were great," and then left quickly.

Millicent looked confident about her appearance in the A group. Buddy, her brother, acted like a nervous magpie on a hot wire. "The class starts in ten minutes. Aren't you supposed to be wearing spurs?"

"Yes, Buddy."
"How about your crop?"
"It's right here."
"Shouldn't you be mounted by now?"
"Buddy, just shut up! Don't say another word."

He looked at his watch, and then trotted over to the groom. "Is Diamond all ready to go?"

Millicent shot him a sour look, bent to strap on her spurs and mounted Black Diamond. "I know he just wants to help, but if he fusses over me one more time, I'll brain him," she muttered. Dime-sized raindrops began to plop onto the dust. She kicked Diamond and trotted to the arena dome with Buddy in pursuit. "Why don't they get some decent music?" she complained. "I'm sick of that cornball organ." She watched the woman who would judge her class being escorted to the center of the arena. "I looked her up this afternoon and went over to introduce myself," she told her brother. "Never hurts to meet the judge—especially if your name is Duke."

Buddy paced, not paying much attention. Millicent stood in her stirrups and peered around the railing, finally spotting Garth. "Wait until I ace this course. Even he's never done that. From now on he's going to stop talking about Amanda and start talking about me."

At last the gate swung open and Black Diamond and Millicent were announced. They galloped into the show ring. Her jaw was squared and her teeth were clenched. The dark gelding raced toward the first jump and hurtled over. Millicent leaned forward across her mount's neck. They streaked across a double oxer, made an abrupt left turn and began a headlong rush toward a brush jump in the center of the ring.

"Too fast. Too fast," Buddy hollered.

Black Diamond had no time to gather himself or set his feet properly. He lowered his head, stiffened his forelegs and came to a sliding halt. They skidded into the jump, sending poles flying. Millicent sailed over the horse's head and landed on the opposite side, still clutching the reins. A collective gasp rose from the spectators.

Millicent leaped to her feet, her face red and twisted with rage. She scrambled over the fallen wooden rails, jerking the reins so hard she nearly knocked the gelding off his feet and raised her crop over his head. At the moment when the audience saw she was unhurt, they started to clap, but the applause dwindled to silence.

"You stupid…" Her voice carried throughout the hushed building. She looked up at the grandstand and her right hand stopped its downward arc. She slowly lowered the riding crop, spun on her heel and paced from the ring. The black horse limped behind her.

Buddy scurried ahead to the stable. Millicent reached into her hip pocket, pulled out a handkerchief and blew her nose. She wiped a drop from her cheek, took a deep breath and led Black Diamond to the stable. When she reached the stall, her brother held the door open. "Take the horse, Buddy." She shouldered him aside, throwing the reins to him and paced down the corridor. Buddy twitched with a spasm, and then stiffened for several seconds.

Millicent headed for McKenzie's stabling area. Her riding crop began to snap against her boot top. When she arrived at Tornado's stall, she glared at the blue ribbon tacked to his stall door.

Amanda looked up. "I'm sorry you fell…" she began, not really meaning it.

"Don't waste your sympathy. I'll be feeling sorry for you before long. Better go home and practice, Amanda. I'm going to beat that big, white horse of yours. He won't look so hot when I get through with him."

Something in her voice made Amanda shiver.

CHAPTER SEVEN

A couple of weeks later, Amanda sat at the kitchen table working on an entry form. Her dad struggled with bookkeeping, muttering to himself. Her mother finished up the dishes, neatly folded the dishtowel and hung it over the hook. At that moment, it happened for the second time.

The girl dropped her pencil, leaped to her feet and knocked her chair over backwards.

Kathy whirled around, "What? What's the matter?"

Jim sprang up, grabbing the floor lamp as it started to fall. Their daughter was rigid, staring into space

"What on earth is wrong with her, Jim?"

Amanda didn't move. Her arms were stiff, fingers splayed, mouth slightly opened, eyes staring. Jim started toward her just as she blinked, shook her head and turned to her parents.

"Fire," she gasped, "the barn's on fire!" At that moment the first piercing shrieks of the horses came from the paddocks.

The family was out the door, across the porch, down the stairs and running to the stables. They rounded the corner and met columns of flame slicing up the sides of the white-frame building. Jim darted into the tack room and dialed the fire department, then raced toward the blaze. Amanda tore the sweater from her shoulders, ducked into the first stall and led a terrified gelding through the flames with the sweater wrapped around the animal's head, shielding his eyes; Kathy led a big mare to safety. They tied the animals to the hitching rail.

Amanda turned and shouted above the roar, "Where's Tornado?" At that moment, she saw her father run down the central aisle, opening each horse's door; saw Tornado leap from his stall and gallop to safety. Still holding the sweater, she ducked into Star's space.

"No, Amanda," shouted her mother.

The smoke was so thick she could hardly make out the shadow that was her mare, cringing in the far corner. She dropped to all fours and crawled through the heat. She could hear the building hissing and sizzling. She felt that each soot-filled breath was strangling her. She heard her mare cough and gasp. The fetid air wrapped around her like a thick, down quilt and closed over her head. She sank into a blistering cradle of darkness.

* * *

Garth was in his room when he heard the wail of the fire engines. He looked up from his desk and listened, trying to hear the direction it came from. He went to the window, opened it and leaned out. The sound was coming closer. He felt the chill of dread any horse breeder, trainer or stable owner feels when he hears that sound. A barn filled with precious animals can vanish in a flash. The front door, which was directly below his room, opened and he heard his parents walk out onto the porch. The scream of the siren grew closer; he saw red lights flashing past on the road, heading south. He listened to the whine fade, but before it had completely died out it stopped. McKenzie's!

He ran into the hall and down the stairs, Pete right behind him. They found their dad searching for the car keys. The sound of a second fire truck shrieked past the house.

A moment later they all leaned forward in the speeding car, its tires squealing up the driveway. The sky glowed orange to the south. It must be a big one, Garth thought.

As they rounded a corner, they saw McKenzie's barn, flames towering skyward. The fire trucks and men formed dark, moving silhouettes against the blaze. Their quick, jerky movements gave the scene a surreal feeling. Jets of water sprayed into the air, sending steam clouds into the night. Horses screamed. Several animals were tied to a rail, pulling against their ropes, thrashing to be free, their eyes wild with terror.

Garth began searching the inferno for Amanda. He found Tornado's great white figure, nervously shifting his hindquarters from side to side, pulling against the rope that held him, trumpeting wildly.

"I wonder if they got all the horses out?" Pete's voice piped.

"We'd never get in there now." Just as he said that, he saw a firefighter plunge from the barn doorway carrying something. He was followed by Jim's bent figure crouching through the flames with a gunny sack over his head. Then he saw Kathy McKenzie rush forward and try to take the burden from the fireman's arms. It was a person he was carrying. It was Amanda!

CHAPTER EIGHT

Amanda's eyelids flickered open. She lay on the grass looking up at the fire-lit sky. Her chest ached. Her throat burned. She began to cough and struggled to sit up, trying to focus. She felt her mother's hand holding hers, saw her father, face blackened and hair singed, kneeling beside her and Garth's face looking over his shoulder, a vein pulsating in his temple. Then she remembered.

"Star?" she whispered. She saw her father look at her mother and shake his head.

The flames lost their battle with the spraying hoses. Pungent odors of wet wood and burned hair hung over the farm. Neighbors stood in subdued groups murmuring quietly to one another while firemen pulled their hoses back to their rigs. The horses were still tied around the yard, nervous and unsure. Dan, the veterinarian, made his way down the line, checking each one. Amanda sat on a low bench with her face in her hands. Garth was crouched in front of her and Pete stood beside him. Jim, Kathy and Mack, the fire chief, talked beside the wreckage that had been their barn.

"Where's Fitz, your hired man?" Mack asked. "I'd like to talk to him."

"It's his night off. Probably in town somewhere."

"I'm going to poke around out here a while. When he comes back, tell him I'd like a word." The chief stared at the ruin. "You only lost the one horse, that right?"

Jim nodded. "Luckily, we never tore down the old stable building. It'll be fine for the horses for a little while."

Within minutes Fitz's small, bowlegged figure jogged down the driveway, his face fixed in a grimace of alarm. His story was that he'd heard about the fire when he came out of the movie theater. "Don't right remember what picture I seen, Guv'nor. Slept clean through it, I did."

"Anyone you know see you?"

"Nary a one, sir." He twisted his cap between gnarled fingers.

"What time'd you leave for town?"

"Right after me supper. Round about six thirty."

"OK, Fitz. I may want a few minutes with you in the morning." Mack turned away and rubbed his hand over his face and sighed.

* * *

The next morning Amanda heard a tap on her bedroom door, it opened and her mother peeped in. The girl rolled over and stretched. "What time is it?"

"Almost ten. How do you feel?" Her mother and father slipped in.

"OK, I think." She tasted smoke. Suddenly it all swept back and the tightness in her chest grew. "How could this happen to our barn? We're always so careful."

Her dad shook his head and walked to the window, pulled the curtain back and glanced out. "Mack's on his way. We'll know something soon." He turned and sat on the sill, arms folded, "Amanda, do you remember last night before the fire started? You went into some kind of trance and then you yelled 'Fire'."

Amanda bit her lip and tried to pull her wits together.

"I don't really know what happens…" she began.

"Happens?" Her mother slowly lowered herself to sit on the edge of the bed. "You mean this has happened before?"

"Remember the day Garth killed a rattlesnake on the trail?" Amanda continued, "It was that day." She described the experience in as much detail as she could remember. She told about Garth's mare bolting and then about the picture of a rattlesnake bursting into her mind. She explained how only Tornado could have seen the snake, but Garth found it right where she said it was. "We talked about it and tried to figure out what was going on. We finally decided I must be getting pictures or messages or something from Tornado. I know it sounds crazy but I'm sure that's what happened last night."

Her mother sat very still with no expression Amanda could read. Her father looked at his daughter a long minute, eyes narrowed in concentration. Finally he said softly, as if to himself, "There's just got to be some other explanation."

The crunch of the Fire Chief's car on the gravel drive broke into their thoughts. Her father looked out and called, "Be right down, Mack." He looked at his daughter again, shook his head and left the room.

* * *

"How's it going? Finding anything?" Jim asked as he walked toward the chief.

"There are a couple of suspicious looking rags. They're so charred I can't say for sure this is arson, but I don't like the look of it."

"Arson! You mean you think someone started this deliberately? You think someone's trying to burn us out? My God, Mack."

"Jim, I don't want to think what I'm thinking, but I'd bet ten to one that's what happened."

Jim sat down heavily on a bench; his hands planted on his knees and stared across the fields. The minutes lengthened. Finally he cleared his throat and said, "Don't tell Kathy or Amanda. You're not sure and I don't want to scare them."

"I'm sure, Jim. In my own mind I'm sure. I think you're making a mistake not telling them. They can handle it and you folks need to have your eyes open 'round here. Someone out there is dangerous."

"Maybe you're right, maybe you're right. I can't take it in yet."

Amanda and Kathy walked out of the house and onto the wide terrace. Kathy put her arm around her daughter's shoulders, "You've got to go down sooner or later, Amanda. The longer you wait, the harder it'll be." The girl nodded.

As they neared the site of the fire, the sharp stench almost made Amanda retch. She saw what used to be the barn. Her father and Mack were at the far end of the rubble, Jim seated and Mack standing with one foot on the bench, left elbow leaning on his cocked knee. They both stared toward the road. Something in the scene made Amanda uneasy. "What's wrong, Dad? Did we lose more horses than we thought?"

The chief answered the girl when her father failed to respond. "Mornin' Amanda, mornin' Kathy. I think I dropped a bomb on your dad, honey."

Jim found his voice. "I'm sorry, I'm just not thinking right. Mack says the fire was set deliberately."

Amanda heard her mother gasp and felt a shiver run through her own body. Somewhere they must have an enemy so filled with hatred that he or she was willing to risk sending fifteen horses to a horrible death. "Are you sure?"

"In my own mind I am. 'Fraid I can't prove it."

"Maybe it's some maniac." Amanda clung to the hope. "We just happened to be in the wrong place at the wrong time."

"Could be. But in case it wasn't a random nut, try to think of someone who might have it in for you."

"You questioned Fitz last night," Jim said. "Did he have any idea what might have happened?"

"Nope, nothing. I may get back to him."

Amanda remembered that their hired man used to work for the Duke family. For an instant she saw Millicent's face, twisted with anger, saying, "That big, white horse of yours won't look so hot when I get through with him."

She shook her head and dismissed the thought.

CHAPTER NINE

Amanda held the telephone receiver to her ear. "I'm sorry, it's hard to hear you over the hammering," she said. A new stable was under construction on the site of the incinerated one. "A swimming party?" She twisted her feet through the rung of the chair. Should I pretend I have something else to do? I wonder if Garth will be there. I haven't seen him since the night of the fire. "Thanks, Millicent, I'd love to come," she replied.

Amanda hung up the phone and began to chew the stub of her pencil. Why is Millicent being nice to me all of a sudden? I'll bet it means trouble. Her frown deepened. She thumbed through the calendar and wrote "swimming party" in for next Thursday. "I'm going to regret this," she murmured.

* * *

Thursday afternoon at ten past one Amanda heard the Duke's chauffeur-driven Cadillac pull into her driveway. She opened the screen door and ran down the stairs. Paul, his sister Lois, and Amanda's good friend, Georgia, already sat inside the long, grey limo. Paul hopped out and held the seat back down so Amanda could climb into the rear. He bounded in beside her, moving close with his arm draped casually across the back of her seat. Next they stopped to pick Garth up. He looked back at them and slid in next to Georgia. He was quiet, none of his usual jokes.

Buddy had obviously been watching for them. The oak door flew open and Buddy ran down the steps, wearing a flowered shirt over his swimming trunks. His hair was slicked back and the teeth of the comb had left little ridges in his hair. He took Amanda's hand in his warm, moist palm. She glanced over at Garth, but he was standing with his back turned, talking to Craig Sutherland.

Half an hour later the girls were spread around on the grass, lying in the sun on their beach towels. Amanda was on her stomach with her fists under her chin talking to Lois and Georgia. Millicent lay on her back with her eyes closed not taking any part in the conversation. Garth, Paul, Craig and Buddy were in the pool playing keep away with a beach ball and inflatable mattress. Laughter bounced off the bath house walls.

Buddy kept looking at Amanda and finally quit the game and pulled himself onto the edge of the pool with his feet dangling in the water. "Come sit by me, Amanda," he said, patting the tiled pool side. She got up and slowly joined him.

Eventually the other boys gave up and flopped onto the edge, panting. Millicent had been waiting. She got up and pushed herself between Paul and Garth, squeezing her body close to Garth's. Amanda strained to hear what they said.

"You look like a blond Tarzan, Garth. How do you think I look?"

"Great, Millicent." Garth didn't move away.

"You should come over to swim more often. By yourself."

Amanda leaned forward a little further to peek around Buddy. She lost her balance and with a splash fell face first into the water. Millicent and Garth began to laugh. "Eavesdropping doesn't pay, Amanda," Millicent said, chuckling.

Amanda swam across the pool and pulled herself up to the edge. Despite the cold water, her face felt hot.

"I'm starved," Millicent said. C'mon girls, help me get some food." They trailed after her to the big house and into the kitchen.

Millicent darted across the room and slammed the door shut. "Don't go into that part of the house," she said. For a moment, Amanda thought Millicent looked frightened.

"Here's a platter, Georgia, put some cold cuts on it," Millicent directed. "There's bread in that roll-out drawer." She threw open the pantry door and pointed to the left, "Amanda, you'll find pickles and mustard and mayo in here. Lois, the cokes are in the fridge beside the storeroom."

Amanda picked up a basket and went into the storage room. She spotted the pickles, picked up a jar and found the mustard. The mayo must be here somewhere, she said to herself. She moved a jar of peanut butter aside and saw something metallic gleam in the dim light. She reached in and pulled out a small, black pistol. Is it a toy, she wondered. She tested its heavy, cold weight in her palm. She wanted to drop it and wipe her hand.

"What are you doing in there?" Millicent called.

"Coming." Amanda put the gun back on the shelf, replaced the peanut butter, picked up the mayonnaise and went back to the kitchen.

"Lois, can you handle the pop and the ice bucket?" Millicent asked.

Lois hung the ice bucket over her right arm and lifted a pack of coke in each hand, "I'm on my way." The door banged behind her.

"I'll take the tray." Amanda's knees still shook as she started for the door.

"Just a sec." Millicent acted as if she had just remembered something. "Come upstairs for a minute. I want you girls to see my new dress." She pushed through the swinging kitchen door.

Amanda looked at Georgia and said, "Us?"

Her friend shrugged her shoulders and lifted both hands, palms up.

"Maybe I am going to find out why I was really invited today," Amanda whispered. The first thing she saw when they trudged up the staircase and through the bedroom door was Garth's picture displayed in a silver frame, smiling from the nightstand beside Millicent's bed. Georgia looked at her, then followed her friend's eyes and caught her breath.

"You noticed the picture," Millicent said. "It's my favorite gift from Garth, especially with this inscription, 'With love to Millicent'." She raised it and held it up, making sure they could read the message in the lower right hand corner. Then she held it to her heart with both hands and twirled around. "Garth is such a dear. He does such loving and thoughtful things."

Millicent put the picture on the dresser and went to the closet for the dress. Amanda tried to blink back the tears and be polite and admire the beautiful dress.

* * *

When they carried the food out, Amanda couldn't eat. She didn't want to look at Garth, but couldn't resist glancing around for him. She leaned over and whispered to Georgia, "Where'd Garth go?"

"Dunno," her friend said around a mouthful of potato salad. "Probably to puke after being with Millicent."

Amanda laughed, maybe too hard. "I knew I shouldn't have come today," she said. Then she had a second thought, maybe it's good I did. Finding that gun makes me sure I'm right about one thing. There's something suspicious going on in this house.

CHAPTER TEN

Laurence Duke sauntered down the curved staircase of his quiet mansion, stopping on the landing to straighten the heavy gold frame of a painting. He stepped back, nodded with satisfaction and continued down. His lean body was dressed in an open-necked, white shirt, cashmere sweater and khaki pants. From the entry hall, he entered his office and pushed the door closed behind him. It was quiet and orderly, as usual. He walked around the desk and seated himself in front of its mahogany work surface. Reaching in the humidor, he took out his first cigar of the day, rolled it between thumb and forefinger, lit it and rocked back in his desk chair, watching the smoke coil toward the ceiling.

After several minutes, he sat forward and opened the lower left desk drawer. He stopped with his hand suspended above it, staring into the drawer. Leaping up, he returned to the doorway, opened it and called, "Millicent, Buddy, get down here right now." He heard the muffled sounds of doors opening, followed by footsteps quickly crossing the upstairs hallway. Laurence Duke returned to his desk, holding the cigar between his teeth, eyes squinted.

Millicent arrived in the doorway first, looking tense; Buddy appeared a few seconds later. Their father nodded toward chairs. When they were seated he leaned back and began, "Who's been in here?" Millicent sat straighter in her chair. Buddy began to squirm. "This drawer's been opened." Beads of perspiration shone on Buddy's upper lip. His father's black eyes fastened on him. "Do you have something to say?"

"N...no. I haven't come near your office. I would never do that. You know I wouldn't. You know I..."

"Stop prattling. If I knew, I wouldn't have asked." He turned to Millicent.

"Don't look at me," she said.

"I heard kids at the pool yesterday."

Millicent and Buddy nodded in unison.

"Anyone get in the house?"

Buddy ran his tongue across his upper lip. "I never set foot in the house all afternoon. I never..."

"Not you. Anyone else?"

"I don't think so."

"Don't you know?"

"Yeah, yeah. I know."

Laurence Duke turned back to his daughter.

"The girls came in to help me get some food. I took them upstairs to my room for a minute. No one went anywhere else."

Her father stared at her for a long moment. "I want the names of everyone who was here yesterday." He passed a sheet of paper and pencil to his daughter. When she had finished writing, he pulled it back and studied it. "Keep kids out of this house from now on." He looked down and resumed leafing through the drawer. "Beat it," he added. When the door closed behind them, he began to curse under his breath. "I must be getting careless. I didn't lock the office door. If anyone got hold of the information in this drawer, and has the brains to know what to do with it, he or she needs to be silenced. Permanently."

***

When Buddy and Millicent reached the safety of the hall, Buddy stumbled and leaned back against the teakwood paneling with his eyes closed.

"What's wrong with you?" Millicent asked.

"It's my head. God it hurts."

"Take an aspirin. Did you notice Garth disappeared for a while yesterday?"

"Uhn-uhn."

"He wasn't at the pool when we brought the eats out. He didn't come back for a while."

"So?"

"I'm not sure." She nodded toward the office door. "Do you think Garth might have gone in there?"

Buddy shrugged.

* * *

That afternoon Millicent headed for their stable. She was smiling. What fun it had been to take Garth away from Amanda. "I knew I could," she congratulated herself. The heels of her boots tapped along the brick paved aisle between stalls. "Bobby, saddle Featherstone." The stable hand jumped. Millicent had a new goal; she meant to beat Amanda and Tornado.

Tornado continued to win every class he entered and his reputation grew in the local press. The Shawnee Valley newspaper ran a story on the front page of the Sports Section, headlined, "Three-Year-Old Stallion Promises Brilliant Future."

Below the article was a quarter-page photo of Amanda riding the big, white horse and clearing a jump with a foot to spare. Millicent had thrown the paper across the room. Now she paced back and forth, slapping her patent-leather boot top. At last Bobby led the bay gelding out of his stall. The animal pranced and danced at the end of his reins. Millicent grabbed them, tugged them over his neck and mounted. This was not to be Featherstone's lucky day.

They trotted off to the covered training ring. Millicent tied the horse to a hitching ring and set up rail fences, English hurdles, stone wall and brush jumps. She remounted, picked up the reins and dug her spurs into Featherstone's flanks.

Approaching the first rail fence, he set his feet and took wing. Next was a picket fence. He had never seen anything like this line of white sticks and, at the last minute, tried to run around it. Millicent yanked his rein, spinning him back.

The sounds of their struggles could be heard for the next hour. The horse grunted with effort, breathing heavily. Millicent barked orders, snapping her whip and occasionally dismounting to reset jumps that had crashed to the ground. When the two returned to the barn, the horse was covered with lather, his head hanging low.

The girl and horse worked daily. Millicent seemed demon-driven and would not let up for a day. She was a demanding trainer, but usually got results. The afternoon before the Lexington Hunter and Jumper Show, Featherstone seemed to float over the toughest obstacles.

"Watch out, Amanda." Millicent threw her crop into the air. "No one can beat me now." The schooling had paid off.

CHAPTER ELEVEN

Garth leaned against an old sugar pine, waiting for the cross-country event in Lexington to begin. He had climbed up a hill above the course where he could see most of the jumps spread below him. He spotted Tornado and Amanda, looking tiny in the distance. She wore a black hunt coat, tan britches, black boots and a black velveteen hunt cap. Tornado's shimmering white body towered over the other horses and Amanda sat straight with her head cocked, listening to last minute announcements. He saw Fitz make an adjustment, then give Tornado a final pat.

"We have a late entry in the next class, Cross Country Hunters. Millicent Duke riding Featherstone." Garth thought about last night's jumper class, when Featherstone had been terrific, turning in a no fault performance. Millicent and Amanda had tied for first place. On the jump off to determine the winner, Featherstone seemed to tire and knocked down a rail. Tornado's second round had been as strong as his first. He won the class. Apparently Millicent had decided to have another try at beating the big, white stallion.

"Maybe she can. Tornado's a high jumper, just what

last night's class was judged on." Garth said to himself. "I've never seen the stallion on a cross country course. I wonder how he'll handle being on a mock fox hunt, with streams, hay bales, barrels and hedges."

The murmur of voices from below grew quiet. The first entrant galloped across the grass and passed the starting flags. The horse and rider flashed through the trees, the man's crimson coat a beacon Garth could follow. They emerged, took the zig-zag fence, turned left over a stream, up the hill to clear a wall, then thundered through a grove of oaks. The sound of hoof beats pounded past him and down the hill. He saw the grey horse and red coated rider in the distance, cantering between fluttering banners and over the finish line.

"Three time faults and four faults for a run out. Ronald Kingman riding Mr. Deeds has seven faults total. Next we have number seventy-two, Millicent Duke riding Featherstone."

The gelding's chocolate coat passed between the flags. Garth watched the two clear the zig-zag and the stream, gallop up the hill, jump the wall and disappear into the trees. In a moment they reappeared, jumped over a pile of barrels, onto a mound with a fence on top. Over the fence they soared and down the other side, cantering toward the last obstacle, a mock pig pen. Featherstone sailed in, took two strides and leaped out the opposite side.

"A perfect performance by Featherstone, Millicent Duke in the saddle," the announcer informed the audience. *Beautiful.* Garth thought. *That's gonna be tough to beat.*

Ten more horses did their best on the course, none with perfect performances. At last he heard, "The final entry is number eighty-four, Amanda McKenzie riding her stallion, Tornado." The huge, white horse galloped onto the grounds. Garth watched them soar over the first fence and cross the stream. He heard Tornado's hoof beats growing louder as the horse and Amanda came up the hill. They cleared the wall and disappeared into the oak trees.

Abruptly the drumming of hoofs stopped. Garth straightened. He stood for an instant, watching for the big horse to emerge from the grove, then he leaped forward, covering the distance to the wooded area at a dead run.

* * *

Amanda had been hurtling through the trees when suddenly her saddle pitched to the left. Tornado felt her weight shift and he swerved, trying to keep his body beneath her, but a tree loomed in front of him and he had to swing sharply to the right. Amanda's face was raked against a limb. It caught her helmet and tore it off. As the saddle came loose, the girl toppled to the left and slammed into the ground, cracking her head on a rock. The stallion fell hard on his side, grunted, then lurched to his feet and shook himself.

Everything was quiet. Tornado moved to stand beside Amanda's still form. He dropped his head and nudged her with his nose. She didn't move. The horse threw his head back and trumpeted, then looked down at the girl and nickered. Still she did not stir. He stamped his front hoof, moved his muzzle across her body, and stood silently over her.

That's how Garth found them. When he burst through the underbrush, Tornado turned toward him with his ears back, guarding Amanda. "Steady, boy. What's the trouble here?" The horse bobbed his head when he recognized Garth. At that moment, the young man saw Amanda's crumpled form lying with one arm flung out and her right leg twisted under her body.

"Amanda!" He was on his knees beside her. He put his head down to listen for her heartbeat. His own heart hammered so loudly he couldn't be sure of hers. She looked like a broken doll lying in the grass, her long lashes on her cheeks and the dark hair curling around her face.

Reaching under her knees with one arm and around her body with the other, he lifted the girl. "Amanda, please open your eyes," he whispered. Sticky, warm blood seeped onto his arm. He started down the hill carrying the girl. Tornado walked slowly behind them.

The announcer broke the silence, "There appears to be trouble at the fifth barrier." Jim McKenzie was running toward the trees with Kathy at his heels. Garth paced out of the woods carrying their daughter, followed by the big white stallion. "Someone's injured. Please get the ambulance up here immediately," said the loudspeaker voice. Amanda's parents raced up to Garth.

"She hasn't moved."

"I'll take her." Jim touched her bloody hair.

"It's OK, I've got her." An ambulance wailed up the hillside. Two white-coated attendants laid a stretcher on the ground and Garth lowered the girl's limp body. The driver and aide lifted it and slipped Amanda into the back. Kathy, Jim and Garth jumped in beside her and the ambulance shrieked out of the show grounds.

Tornado stood alone on a rise, head held high with the breeze ruffling his mane. He whinnied from deep within his chest, the sound starting low, rising to a shrill cry that rang across the grounds. A hush fell over the crowd watching the stallion on the hill, silhouetted against the sky. A small figure approached the horse with his hand out. Peter Bannock took Tornado's reins and led him to the barns.

* * *

Garth looked at the hospital waiting room clock. The hands didn't seem to move. Jim sat on a naugahyde sofa staring at the green tile floor. He leaned forward with his elbows on his knees, head resting in his hands. Garth picked up a magazine, then put it down again and ran his fingers through his hair. Kathy came down the hall carrying coffee none of them could drink.

"They must know something by now," Jim said.

Garth looked up, startled by Jim's voice. His mind had been far away. He turned back to stare out the window, put his forearm across the sash and rested his head against the cool glass. He watched a robin on the lawn below, cocking its head in the same way Amanda did. He remembered the lopsided birthday cake she had baked for him, the time the two of them built a raft to sail to the sea, the expression on her face the morning she held his hand and took him to see her new foal, Tornado.

Footsteps echoed down the corridor and Garth's parents, Phil and Greta Bannock came around the corner, trailed by Peter. "Any news?"

Jim shook his head.

"Tornado's fine. Fitz'll take care of your horses at the show grounds tonight. We'll stop by your place on our way home and see to your other animals," Garth's father said. He stopped talking and stood in the middle of the room. "Oh, and we went up into the woods and got Amanda's saddle. The girth strap broke, that's what caused the accident. We have it in the trunk of the car."

Another hour crawled by before the doctor walked into the room. "Are you the girl's family?" Jim jumped to his feet and the doctor extended a hand. "We've checked her over thoroughly. Her right leg is broken. There's a severe concussion, but no fracture of her skull. No sign so far of any internal damage, but we'll know more in the morning. There's no point in you staying longer. She's sedated; she'll sleep through the night."

The doctor put one arm around Kathy, the other around Jim and walked them to the door. Greta and Phil walked behind. Garth stopped for a moment, turning to stare toward Amanda's door. Peter took his hand and led him down the corridor.

* * *

The next morning Kathy and Jim arrived at the hospital before eight. Amanda was almost as pale as the sterile sheets. Her right leg was in a cast, suspended a few inches above the bed in a sling, her left eye was purple and swollen, her face was scratched and there was a wide gauze bandage wrapped around her head with a red stain spreading across its surface.

"Amanda, darlin'," Kathy whispered.

"Mom?"

"Hi Sweetie," Jim bent to kiss her. Amanda had closed her eyes again and was no longer with them.

An hour later there was a gentle tap-tap and Garth's blond head poked around the door. He stood looking down at Amanda. "She looks like she's been beaten." He ran the back of his hand across his cheek.

Kathy put her arm around his shoulders. "The doctor says she got through the night well."

Jim jumped up. "Here, sit in this chair. I need to get out of here for a while."

Garth rubbed his hand over his face again and took a deep breath. "Can I talk to both of you for a minute?" He motioned toward the hall. "You remember last night when Mom and Dad said they had Amanda's saddle in their trunk?" The McKenzie's nodded. "I looked at it this morning. The girth was sliced almost clear through by something—or someone."

Kathy stared at him.

Jim's face looked exhausted. "Someone? I guess I should take it to Sheriff Clark. I'm probably too suspicious, but after the fire…" His voice trailed off. "My God, what is happening to us?"

CHAPTER TWELVE

Amanda sat on the terrace at home, dozing in the morning sunshine. Darkened glasses partially hid her battered face. Her right leg rested on the lounge chair, wrapped in a plaster cast from thigh to ankle. The morning's newspaper lay scattered on the glass-topped table and wooden crutches leaned against the back of a wrought iron chair. She heard the sound of tires turning in at the gravel driveway and sat up, shading her eyes with both hands. Garth's old, Ford pick-up rattled up to the porch with the voice of Hank Williams blasting Hey, Good Lookin' on the radio. He'd been driving around his folk's ranch hauling hay, tack and tools since he was twelve.

"Hi, Lazy Bones," he called, snapping off the radio. He jumped out of the truck.

"You're driving. On the road, I mean."

"Yeah." He flashed a wide grin.

"I can't wait to be sixteen."

"I'll take you for a ride as soon as you'll fit in. When do you get that thing off your leg?"

"Four more weeks."

He carefully lowered himself to the edge of her

lounge chair, "Boy, you sure have a colorful face—yellow, red, purple, even a little green."

"I…" Amanda started to tell him how glad she was to see him but remembered the picture in Millicent's bedroom and changed the subject. "Have you seen this morning's paper?"

He reached across her and picked it up.

"The sports page has an article about the accident. The writer hints that it might not have been an accident."

"Unh." He found the section and rustled the paper open, scanning the page. "Yeah. None of us wanted to scare you when you were so sick, but," Garth cleared his throat, "your saddle strap was purposely cut."

Amanda felt the small hairs on the back of her neck rise.

"Your Dad took it to Sheriff Clark. The police lab said it was sliced almost clean through from underneath, so when you saw it, it looked OK. They didn't know what the person used, probably a pocket knife."

She looked at him for several seconds, glad her eyes were hidden behind the glasses.

Garth stood up and walked to the edge of the porch with his hands in the pockets of his jeans, "I want to find out what's going on before anything else happens to you." He half turned toward her. "Remember the swimming party at Buddy and Millicent's?"

Boy, do I, she thought.

"I sneaked into Mr. Duke's office that day. Nothing was lying around on the desk so I started looking into the drawers."

Amanda caught her breath. "What'd you find?"

"There's something fishy over there. The name "Tornado" was written over and over on a pad of paper, like doodling." Garth frowned in concentration. "Why would Laurence Duke be interested in your horse? I've gotta go back. I ran out of time."

"Garth, be careful. I saw a gun in their house the day of the party."

* * *

The following week, Amanda hobbled to classes on crutches and became the center of attention for a few days. Her friends covered her cast with scrawled jokes and messages. There wasn't a blank half inch anywhere on the dirty white plaster when the time came to have it cut off.

A new barn took shape on the site of the ravaged one. Meanwhile, Tornado had a holiday and spent playful afternoons under the oak trees. When Amanda hobbled out to visit him, he delighted in showing off for her. He careened across the fields, racing up to fences, stiffening his legs and skidding to a halt at the last possible moment, inches from the rails. He whirled and thundered back across the pasture, his silvery mane and tail flowing. He kicked his heels in the air and twisted his body like a bronco. Again he spun and trotted back to her, flinging his front legs out at every step. With each stride, his body seemed to hang suspended for a moment above the earth.

She clapped and cheered after each performance.

* * *

Amanda mended at last. She and Tornado graduated to the top division in the show ring, where they continued to win every class they entered. Before the shows, Jim went to the tack room and inspected each piece of equipment Amanda planned to use. Satisfied there had been no foul play, he stationed himself in front of the door with folded arms. There were no more incidents.

Amanda and her amazing stallion continued to burn up the show ring with their performances. The pair grew accustomed to the brilliant flashes of reporter's cameras. The Shawnee Valley Bugle wrote about Amanda McKenzie and Tornado. The article caught the attention of the Lexington Sun, then the Louisville and Cincinnati papers picked it up. The whole region began to talk about "The White Whirlwind Named Tornado."

* * *

Peter was pinning his new third place ribbon to Bannock's tack room door when Amanda came over and put her arm around his shoulders. "I'm proud of you, Peter. You're going to be as good a rider as your brother."

Amanda couldn't think of a better compliment. Peter beamed.

Georgia hurried down the center aisle of the stable, heading for Amanda like a homing pigeon. "You and Tornado were spectacular." She began to giggle. "Millicent Duke's face always looks like curdled milk when you win." Turning to Peter, she added, "I don't know how your brother could possibly like her."

"He doesn't."

"He gave her his picture with some stupid love message written on it."

Amanda made a 'shhhh' motion with her lips.

"What're you talkin' about?" Peter turned from Georgia to Amanda and back again. "Don't shush her, Amanda. I'm not a baby. What'd Garth do?"

Georgia pretended not to notice Amanda trying to quiet her. "Amanda and I saw Garth's picture in Millicent's room and he'd written some mushy stuff on it."

"No, he didn't. I know he didn't"

"Forget it, Peter," Amanda said. "It's not important."

* * *

Garth rode back to the barns after his open hunter class and found Peter waiting for him at the stall door. "How'd you do?" Peter asked. Garth held up a red ribbon. Peter glanced at it, but couldn't hold it in any longer, couldn't even wait until his brother dismounted. "Georgia says you gave Millicent Duke a picture and wrote some love stuff on it," he blurted out.

Garth threw his leg over his mount and dropped to the ground. "Slow down there, old man, what're you talking about?"

* * *

Garth stopped first at the Duke stabling area. "Millicent, I want to talk to you." Ten minutes later he and Millicent marched into Tornado's stall. Garth gave Millicent a push on the shoulder, "Tell Amanda what you did."

"Oh, for heaven's sake, it was only a joke." Millicent tossed her hair. "Don't make a big deal out of nothing."

"Tell her." Garth's jaw clenched.

"I got Garth's picture from school, had it framed and copied his handwriting. I told you it was just a joke." She looked at Amanda and laughed. "You should have seen your face when you saw it. It was worth all the effort." She spun on her heel and stormed out.

Garth turned to Amanda, "You thought I was seeing Millicent all this time and you never said anything?"

Amanda tried to answer, but her lips trembled

"I shoulda told you what I was doing." Garth looked down at the straw. "But I was kinda mad for a while."

"Mad?"

"Every time I saw you with Paul it bugged me. I guess I was jealous. I wanted to show you how it felt."

Amanda didn't know whether she wanted to laugh or cry

"I'm really sorry. It was a pretty stupid thing to do." He put his hands on her shoulders and looked down at her. "There was another reason I hung around with Millicent. I wanted to get back into the Duke house."

Amanda tried to follow the conversation, but her mind was spinning. Garth wasn't dating Millicent! She felt a surge of happiness and knew her eyes were brimming. At last she managed to answer, "You already told me about searching her dad's office."

"I know, but I went back again." He turned toward Tornado, put his hand on the horse's shoulder and said, "Mr. Duke's tied in with a big crime syndicate. One of their operations is gambling on sports events." He glanced at Amanda, trying to gauge her reaction. "One of the things I saw was a newspaper article in a drawer under some papers. It told about a boxer who got shot during a workout in his gym. He had refused to take a dive for the syndicate in a fight they wanted him to throw. Someone called him to the phone on a pretext and shot him. Dead."

Amanda gasped.

"I went to the Sheriff, but I didn't have any proof. I didn't want to take anything out of Mr. Duke's office, I was afraid he would notice it missing. Ed said he couldn't do anything without more to go on, but he'd keep his eyes and ears open."

"Oh, Garth, what if he finds out you were in there snooping?"

"I left everything just exactly as it was. No way he could find out. Well, except…"

"Except what?"

"Millicent knows."

CHAPTER THIRTEEN

The sun was beginning to peep over the horizon when Amanda woke from a troubled dream. For the first time in months, she couldn't feel Tornado's spirit within her. She threw on jeans and a sweatshirt, slipped into loafers and ran down the stairs, almost falling on the terrace. She stopped to tug a loafer back over her heel, and then tripped again on the stone steps as she ran.

Tornado's dark eyes didn't watch for her when she came around the corner. The girl raced up and looked over his door; he stood at the far side of the stall with his head drooping to the ground, his labored breathing making a soft, wheezing sound.

Amanda opened the stall door and ducked under the rope. The stallion showed no sign of seeing her. She touched his sides and felt the effort of each breath against his ribs. The girl ran back to the house, shouting for her mother and father even before she reached the porch, then stumbling through the screen door, still calling.

Her mother hurried down the stairs, slippers flapping, "What on earth's wrong?"

"Tornado's sick."

Amanda's father was right behind her mother, tucking in his shirt. "Call the vet, Kathy. I'm going out to have a look."

When Amanda and Jim reached Tornado's stall, her father ran his hands over the horse's body and down his legs. He put his ear to Tornado's chest, listening to the animal's labored lungs. "His breathing passages are clogged but he doesn't seem to have a fever."

Amanda stood in front of her horse, holding his head between her hands. "He's so sick, Dad."

"He sure is. I wonder why Fitz didn't notice an hour ago when he fed the horses."

The two busied themselves trying to ease Tornado's suffering until Dan's pick up pulled into the yard. The door slammed and the vet ran down the lawn straight to the big horse's stall. "Hi there, Tornado, what seems to be the trouble?"

The veterinarian went to work. Twenty minutes later he turned, wiping his hands on a towel. "I can't find a darn thing. It sounds like a lung infection but there's no temperature." He rested his chin on his knuckles and studied the animal. "I'm stumped; never saw an infection without a temp." The vet began to roll down his sleeves while he went on, "I've taken a couple of blood samples and I'll drive them over to the lab in New Bend. We need a rush job on this." Amanda couldn't remember ever seeing Dan look so worried.

The vet rummaged through his bag and extracted a hypodermic needle. "I'm going to give him a shot that should help a little." He grabbed a handful of skin on the horse's neck and plunged the needle in. Tornado didn't flinch. Dan repacked his bag, picked up each blood sample, capped it and placed it in a wooden carrier. His movements were quick and tense.

A sickening wave of terror began to build in Amanda's chest.

"It'll take me about three hours to drive each way, but you know how to reach me." He loped up to the truck and sped away, turning out of the drive as Garth's pick-up turned in at the gate.

When Garth got to the barn, he took one look at the stallion and said softly, "My God."

Amanda closed her eyes and tried to catch her breath, and to keep her body from trembling.

"Until we know something, one of us better stay

with Tornado every minute," her father said. "I want to be sure no one gets near him. This could be a poisoning.

* * *

Garth, Jim and Kathy were in and out of the stallion's stall all day, but Amanda didn't leave Tornado's side. In early afternoon, the shot Dan had given the animal kicked in. The horse's breathing eased and he raised his head and walked to Amanda. She had been at her horse's side all day, stroking his neck, combing his mane with her fingers, whispering to him that they were going to make him better soon. By the time Dan returned from New Bend, the stallion was again wheezing and gasping for every breath.

"The lab promised to give us first priority," the vet tried to sound positive. "How'd this big guy's day go?" Amanda filled him in. Dan gave the horse another shot and stood looking at him for several seconds, absently jingling the change in his pocket. At last he walked up the lawn, frowning and shaking his head.

Amanda straightened her spine. Be brave for Tornado, she told herself.

Jim decided two people should guard the stallion through the night. At ten-thirty he and Garth finally convinced Amanda to go to bed, promising they would wake her if Tornado changed for the better or worse. She fell into a deep sleep the moment she laid her head on the pillow.

At four a.m. she bolted upright, wide awake. In her mind she could see every detail of Tornado's stall. The water bucket hung just inside the double door, as usual. The top half of the door cracked open a couple of inches. An arm darted through and emptied a white packet into the bucket, then withdrew rapidly.

Amanda shot out of bed. Now she felt certain Tornado had been poisoned and whoever did it had come back to finish him off. The girl ran toward the barn, trying to shove her arms into the sleeves of her robe. When she burst into the stallion's stall, she found her dad sitting on the straw, leaning against the outside wall, facing away from the door.

"I know what's wrong with Tornado," she gasped.

Garth sat up, rubbing his eyes and brushing hay from his hair. Tornado looked at her and nickered softly. "I got the message you sent me, Tornado." She grabbed her father's arm, "Dad, someone put something from a white packet into Tornado's water bucket. I saw it as clear as I see you. Just five minutes ago."

"Amanda, I've been sitting here wide awake. Don't you think I would have seen someone come into the stall?"

"No, dad. The top door was open a little and whoever did it just shoved his hand through, emptied an envelope into the bucket, and pulled back." She turned to Garth. "The person had on something brown or tan with long sleeves."

"Maybe we ought to take a sample of the water and scrub the bucket, just in case," Garth said. Amanda knew he believed her.

"I guess it couldn't hurt, but Darlin,' I really think you dreamed it."

Despite Jim's doubts, they filled a mason jar with a sample of water from the horse's bucket, then scrubbed it out and poured fresh water for him.

In the morning Jim phoned the vet, "Dan, Amanda thought she saw something suspicious last night. I'd like to have some water analyzed, along with the blood sample."

"Sure thing," Dan answered. "There's a courier service I can catch if I have your sample ready by nine. Might be able to get the results later today—tomorrow for sure."

"I'll run it over right now." Jim left with the Mason jar and Garth and Amanda sat in the stall, talking quietly.

"You sure look beat," Garth said. Amanda leaned against the rough cedar stall with her eyes closed. "I wish Tornado had seen who it was last night," Garth went on.

"Do you think Millicent could do something this wicked?" Amanda asked without opening her eyes.

"It's hard to think that anyone could, but someone did."

"Maybe they just wanted to make Tornado sick."

Garth shook his head. "That's wishful thinking, Amanda. Every horse in the barn would be dead if you hadn't discovered the fire as early as you did. Cutting your cinch could've killed you." His voice deepened. "This game's gone beyond warnings. It is deadly now."

They heard Fitz's footsteps padding up and down between the stalls. Hay rustled and his voice mumbled occasionally. His weathered face appeared in the doorway, "'Ow's the patient this mornin'?"

"About the same, I guess," Amanda answered.

"Will I gi' 'im some hay, then?"

"You can try a fresh flake."

He busied himself carrying out her instructions. Amanda tapped Garth's arm and nodded toward Fitz. The man wore a brown sweater.

* * *

The second day of Tornado's illness seemed endless. The stallion drank a great deal of the carefully watched water and managed a few nibbles of hay; otherwise he remained listless and largely unresponsive to anyone but Amanda. When she was with him, he moved to be near her, putting his head over her shoulder or standing so that his body touched hers. She stayed close, talking to him constantly, forcing herself to stay up beat. "I know you can tell what I'm thinking, so I'll never have a doubt and I won't be afraid," she promised her horse. "As soon as you're well, we'll take a picnic into the pasture. I'll make oat and molasses cakes for you. Garth will come with us and we'll play in the sunshine. As soon as you're well." She stroked him, "as soon as you're well," she repeated. Her voice dropped to a whisper, "as soon as you're well."

At five o'clock Dan came again. "Nothing new to report," he told them. "I called the lab a few minutes ago. They're going to work late tonight on the water and blood samples. Should have news by early tomorrow morning."

"We've got a plan for tonight." Jim was tight faced. "There'll be two of us with Tornado every minute, both of us staying awake. We have a wire we're going to rig up that'll sound an alarm if anyone steps within four feet of the door. Until we know for sure, we're going to act like this is a poisoning."

Dan nodded. "Let's have a look at him." The vet spent ten minutes in the stall. When he came out, his face looked bleak. "He's a darned sick animal. I hate this waiting. I can't do a thing to help him until I know what we're fighting. It's important to keep him on his feet; if he tries to lie down, don't let him. If he goes down, he may never get up."

Amanda's knees buckled and for an instant she felt she might go down and never get up, either.

"I'm sorry, folks," Dan went on. "I probably shouldn't have said that. At least, I should have thought of a better way to say it."

Kathy and Jim took the first shift at six.

Garth drove home, thinking grim thoughts. He climbed the stairs and opened the door to his room. A wall of hot, still air met him. He opened his window, lay down on his bed and tried to sleep. Finally he dropped off, only to leap awake from a dream in which he hurtled down a river at flash-flood stage, swept toward a waterfall. He saw Tornado's white body ahead of him with Amanda clinging to his mane; watched both of them plunge over the precipice and then felt himself swept after them, falling, falling... His own shout of alarm woke him.

He got up and showered and drove back to McKenzie's. He and Amanda took the midnight to six a.m. shift. Somehow the night passed. Shortly after six, the two young people traded places with Jim and straggled into McKenzie's kitchen, sinking into chairs while Kathy heated the griddle.

The sharp shrill of the phone made them jump. For an instant they stared at one another, frozen, and then Kathy reached for the receiver. "Hello. Yes, Dan, we've been waiting." After a pause, "I see. OK, we'll look for you in a minute. Thanks." She hung the phone up and turned. "The sample of water from the bucket contained a toxin. They found the same stuff in the blood sample. Tornado's been poisoned."

* * *

Dan's pick up drove into the yard a few minutes later. He trotted down to the stable where he found Jim in Tornado's stall. "Good news for a change. I've got an antidote for the poison." He went to work again. "I guess you know I've got to report this to the Sheriff."

"He won't be surprised," Jim said. "The fire chief

called him when our barn burned and then we took Amanda's girth to him to get confirmation that it was cut, which could lead to an attempted murder charge. The Sheriff's been working on the case, but I guess he hasn't learned much."

Dan stood and slapped Tornado on the rump. "That'll do it for now. You should notice a difference in a couple of hours. It's a good thing he's such a big, strong horse. The dose in his water could have killed him." Dan picked up his bag and turned to Jim. "If word leaks out that he's not dead, someone'll probably come back to finish him off."

Jim nodded, "When you talk to the Sheriff, I'd appreciate it if you'd ask him to be quiet about this. I'd like the killer to think we don't know he's been poisoned."

Sheriff Clark called within the hour. He took a dim view of people trying to play detective on their own. "You're dealing with a dangerous situation here, Jim, not one for amateurs. I don't want to see you get in over your head. I'll be there shortly."

He arrived before noon in an unmarked car. Amanda's father was waiting and led him down to the barn. He showed the Sheriff a wire he had rigged, "If anyone comes within four feet of Tornado's door a buzzer goes off."

"Looks pretty ingenious. I 'spose you've tested it."

"Works like a charm. We're pretty sure the poisonings happen at night. One of us stays with Tornado through the day and at night we double up."

"I'll be here, too." Ed's voice was firm. "I'll hide my car up the road and walk back. Is there an empty stall I can use?"

"We'll find one. I've gotta admit, I'm going to feel a whole lot better knowing you're around, Ed."

* * *

By five o'clock all was in readiness. Dan came back and found Tornado looking more alert than he had for days; he'd even nibbled a few oats. His four guardians were beginning to look a little hollow eyed, however. Fitz puttered about doing his usual chores. If he noticed anything unusual, he gave no sign.

Garth and Amanda were taking the first watch from six to ten. There was a baseball bat hidden in the straw at Amanda's feet and Garth had a thick wooden club. They set the alarm at the door and settled in for a four hour shift. About eight they thought they heard Ed creep into the stall, and then there was complete silence. At ten o'clock Jim and Kathy arrived and tiptoed in. Garth gave them a thumbs-up and they traded places.

Amanda lay on her quilt, staring at the ceiling and trying to sleep. She heard sounds she did not remember hearing before and got up to look out the window three times before she fell into a tormented sleep. When the clock's buzzer went off, in her dream it became the alarm in front of her stallion's stall and she was on her feet before she knew where she was. Her heart pounded with a feeling of foreboding.

Amanda and Garth began the familiar routine once more. She fought the urge to close her eyes. Her head felt heavy and it seemed as though she hadn't slept through the night for a week. She hunched her shoulders and rubbed the back of her neck. Tornado put his head down against her.

Suddenly his head jerked up, ears cocked toward the door. Amanda stopped breathing. Did something rustle? She strained to see Garth, but couldn't be sure she had found him in the dim light. Slowly she began to let her breath out, then she thought she heard a scraping sound, so faint it could have been her imagination.

Tornado stood still as a statue, focused on the doorway.

The alarm went off with a harsh bleep!

Garth's dark shape jumped from the hay, made a grab for his club and missed it, then hurtled through the door and pounded across the lawn. Amanda grabbed her bat and tore after him. She could make out his shadowy form chasing something up the slope, saw him leap to tackle the phantom figure. There was a brilliant flash of gunpowder and the sharp crack of a gunshot echoed through the still night air.

Garth spun backward, fell heavily on the grass and lay still.

CHAPTER FOURTEEN

Amanda ran up the lawn and swung her bat with all her strength. She felt it glance off the head of the fleeing person in front of her and then heard Ed's footsteps racing up the slope.

Lights came on in the house. The next minute the outdoor switch was thrown and the entire stable area blazed in light. A figure lay face down near the top of the incline with Ed kneeling beside it, buckling handcuffs.

Amanda paid no attention to who it might be. She turned and ran back down to Garth. Tornado trotted from the open stall door and stood with his head lowered, touching the young man's body. Amanda dropped to her knees beside them. Garth's eyes opened and he tried to raise his head. Gently she pressed his forehead down. It felt damp and cold. "Please, don't let him die. Oh please, please don't let him die."

Kathy and Jim ran across the lawn. "Dear God, Garth's been shot," Kathy screamed.

Jim dropped to one knee beside them, pulled out his handkerchief and began to dab at the face wound.

"I'm OK," Garth said in a thick voice.

Ed grabbed his two way radio and called for two ambulances, then ran down the incline. "Lay back, son, let's take a look at you."

They stemmed the cheek wound, and pressed a cloth

against Garth's shoulder. "Looks like he'd just launched himself at the killer when the bullet grazed his face and hit him in the shoulder," Ed said.

Garth kept struggling to get to his feet and finally Jim and Amanda helped him up. He stood, leaning against Tornado's flanks. "Did we get 'im?"

"We sure did," Ed said. "At least you and Amanda did. She pasted him one with her bat. He should be out for a while."

"Who is it?"

Amanda put Garth's good arm over her shoulder and helped him walk up to the still form. Ed rolled him over.

"Buddy Duke!" Laurence Archibald Duke III lay unconscious at their feet.

***

The next morning Amanda heard the clock on the landing chime six, threw back the blankets and gave up on sleeping. She got out of bed and went to the window and stood, staring out, thinking about Garth and Tornado. How close she had come to losing both of them. What an incredible few weeks it had been, and now that it was over, why did she still feel a knot in the pit of her stomach? She sighed, turned from the window, dressed and went out to see her stallion.

When she returned to the house, she found her parents seated at the kitchen table drinking coffee and talking. Her dad looked up. "Mornin' Honey. The big guy's looking pretty good today."

"Lots better. Any news?"

"The Sheriff just called. When he left here last night, he went to the hospital. Too early to be sure, but Ed thinks Buddy needs psychiatric help." Jim looked down at the coffee mug cradled between his palms and shook his head. "I guess he's rambling—not making sense. He keeps saying he did it for his father. For some reason he thinks his father will be proud of him."

"What does that mean?"

"Wish I knew." Jim rubbed his hand over his face "Maybe nothing."

"Did Buddy set fire to the barn and cut my cinch?"

Jim shrugged. "Don't know yet." He continued to stare into his cooling coffee.

"Have you called the hospital to see how Garth is this morning?"

Jim came out of his reverie. "Yep." His face broke into a grin. "He's going to be fine, coming home today. Like we thought last night, the bullet grazed his cheek and went through the fleshy part of his shoulder just as he crouched to leap at the gunman."

Amanda suddenly felt exhausted and dropped into a chair, "Tornado's getting well, Garth's going to be OK. Is it over, Dad?"

Her father shook his head, "I wish I could believe it." He stared out the window.

* * *

When Garth came home from the hospital it was to a frequently ringing telephone. The Bugle ran a front page article about Tornado with pictures of Garth and Amanda. The piece reviewed the events of the past year and detailed the climactic night of the shooting, stressing the bravery of the two young people and making them sound like heroes. The name of the shooter was not mentioned, only stating that he was mentally disturbed.

"Hey, this is great." Garth's broad smile made him grimace. "Ow! I guess it only hurts when I laugh."

"It's kinda embarrassing. I don't feel like the fearless person they're writing about." Amanda was sitting in the Bannock's kitchen, watching Garth eat breakfast.

"I think it's neat. Let's enjoy our five minutes of fame. Probably never happen again." His eyes were laughing even though his face couldn't manage it.

It turned out to be a lot more than five minutes of fame. Their story combined mystery and danger, bravery, the romance of young love and a beautiful white stallion who jumped like a soaring comet. It had everything. The Associated Press picked it up; by mid afternoon Jim and Kathy and the Bannocks had been contacted by *Life Magazine*, the *New York Times*, CBS, NBC, ABC, the *Today Show* and *Movietone News*. Over the next few days there seemed to be television crews and news people everywhere they turned. Garth still wore a bandage and sling which made the photos more dramatic. They saw themselves on television; their faces stared out of newsstands and even in movie theaters, where they were featured on newsreels.

CHAPTER FIFTEEN

Jim thought of a way to thank Garth for putting his life at risk for them. When he talked it over with Kathy, she was thrilled.

"What a wonderful idea! Why didn't I think of it? Garth is like our own son and I couldn't be happier."

"You don't have all the good ideas around here, you know. How do you think Amanda will feel about it? I didn't want to mention it to her 'till I found out what you thought."

"She'll be excited, believe me. Can't you tell how she feels about him?"

"It is pretty obvious, isn't it? I guess we all think a whole lot of that boy."

After dinner Jim told Amanda what they were thinking about. She jumped to her feet and clapped her hands. "Oh, Dad, I can't believe it. I love you for thinking of it." She ran to him and put her arms around his neck. "When can we tell Garth?"

"I thought it would be fun to make a production out of it. Let's all go out to dinner at Dominique's. We'll get all gussied up and invite his parents, Phil and Greta, too. We'll tell them it's just a little celebration."

The date was set for Friday night. Amanda and Kathy decided they needed new dresses and came home with shopping bags filled. Amanda thought she would burst waiting for it to be Friday. It came at last. The McKenzie's were to pick up the Bannocks and Amanda and Garth would come separately.

Amanda allowed herself a whole hour to dress. She started with a bubble bath. Feeling luxurious, she dressed slowly, pulling on nylons and slipping into her new heels. The dress was red and styled simply with a short skirt. It made her feel a bit wicked. Her hair was shining and loose, curling down below her shoulders. She put on a little lipstick and a touch of blush. Her spectacular eyes needed no makeup. Lastly, she added the diamond earrings that had been her great grandmother's. She looked in the mirror and smiled at her reflection.

The sounds of her folks leaving drifted up the stairs as Garth's pick-up pulled into the drive. He took the front steps two at a time and called, "Where are you, slowpoke?"

"Coming." She walked slowly down, conscious of the effect she would have; maybe a little self conscious, too.

"Wow!" Garth stood staring at her. He didn't move or speak.

"Do you like it? I hoped you would. It's new."

"I've never seen anyone so beautiful."

With that great beginning, the evening just got better and better. When they arrived at the restaurant, a valet dashed up and helped them from the newly washed pick-up, then parked it. They found their folks at the table and Garth pulled a chair out for Amanda with his good arm. When they were settled, Jim stood up and proposed a toast,

"To the six of us and to a friendship we treasure." Glasses clinked amid murmurs of agreement. "Folks, I told you that tonight was to be a celebration. Actually there's a little more to it."

Amanda reached under the table and took Garth's hand.

Jim turned to look at the young man wearing a white bandage on his cheek. "Garth, I can't begin to tell you what it has meant having you here to help us through this. You risked your life for us without giving it a second thought. We have hoped to find some way to tell you how grateful we are."

Amanda squeezed Garth's hand.

"I believe we have found a way to tell all of you how we feel. Last week I had Tornado's registration papers changed. They now read, owners: Katherine McKenzie, James McKenzie, Amanda McKenzie and Garth Bannock, as equal partners. He belongs to you now, Garth, as much as to any of us."

PART TWO
THE ADVENTURE

CHAPTER ONE

Tornado, "The Magical Horse with Wings on his Feet" continued to win every event he entered. People began to recognize the green and white van marked "McKenzie Stables" when it passed. A few honked and waved, some held up their thumbs or made a victory sign with two fingers.

One evening after Amanda and her dad had stowed the tack, they walked back to the house side by side. "Dad, I've been thinking.

"Oh-oh."

"Have you ever considered entering Tornado in the Worldwide Championship competition in Montreal?"

"Follow me." Jim led the way through the kitchen and into his office. He snapped on the lamp, went to his desk and pulled out a sheet of paper. With a flourish, he handed it to Amanda.

"An entry form? Are we really going?"

"I'd sure like to. Let's get a map out and figure how far it is."

The next morning the phone rang. Amanda was in the barn with Tornado, brushing and polishing him and talking to him about the trip to Montreal, Canada. On the fourth ring she dropped the brush and ran to the tack room phone and picked it up.

"Amanda, this is Millicent."

Amanda felt a stab of baseless fear. "Hi, Millicent."

"I need to talk to you and Garth. Can you meet me today?"

"I guess so," Amanda answered cautiously.

"Make it two-thirty at the Downtown Café." The line went dead.

* * *

At two-thirty Garth and Amanda walked into the diner. Lunch hour was over and the place was deserted except for a booth in the back where they saw Millicent peer out and motion to them. They walked back and slid into the seat, facing her.

Millicent took a deep breath, opened her mouth, and then closed it again, continuing to stare at the table top. Her face was pale and drawn.

Amanda broke the silence. "How's Buddy?"

Millicent looked up for a moment, then shook her head and looked down again.

"Where is he?" Amanda asked, wondering if he was in jail.

"In the Spring Hills Sanitarium. I'm not sure he knows where he is. He doesn't even know he did anything wrong." Millicent continued in a flat voice. "He's had headaches for months. Real bad ones, but I never paid any attention. Looking back, I remember he acted weird, too." Millicent straightened and put both palms flat on the table. "He must have had a gun stashed somewhere."

Amanda remembered the pantry.

Millicent began smoothing her palms across the table top. "I guess in some goofy way he thought he'd get in good with Pop."

"I don't understand," Amanda said.

"I know Buddy heard Pop say he wished your horse was out of the way." Millicent's voice became more intense. "But there's a lot more. That's the reason I wanted to see you. Buddy and I snooped around and finally figured out what Pop does."

A waitress sauntered up and plunked three glasses of water on the table. "What'll you have, kids?"

"Black coffee," Millicent said

Amanda glanced up. "A coke, please."

"Make it two." Garth looked impatient.

The waitress left and Millicent continued, "Pop's a big shot in a crime syndicate. They make big bucks taking bets on a lot of different stuff. Sports betting's a part of it."

"I still don't see."

"Tornado's too good. I finally figured out even I can't beat him. I don't think anyone can."

"You mean when Tornado's entered in a show, no one will bet against him?" Garth asked.

"No one but a nut would bet against him. Buddy thought Pop wanted to get rid of him. But that's not all there is to it."

The waitress returned and slid cokes in front of Garth and Amanda. She shoved a cup of coffee at Millicent, sloshing it over the rim. "Oh-oh, Honey. I'll get you another saucer."

"Just leave it."

"Have it your way, deary." The waitress left.

"Now that Buddy's..." Garth paused and started again. "I mean, do you think Tornado's still in danger?"

Millicent looked at Garth. "You all are. You know too much. Pop found out you got into his office—TWICE!"

"Would your Father?"

Millicent interrupted, "They stop at nothing. None of them. I've been keeping my ears open lately and I've overheard things. Football players in accidents, a Grand Prix driver killed."

Amanda noticed that Millicent's palms left sweaty spots on the table.

"Bad stuff goes on. Watch yourselves. They don't care who gets in their way. I know they wouldn't stop at killing all of you. They think you are a threat—you know too much. They'll make it look like an accident."

Amanda and Garth sat very quietly, their cokes untouched. After a long, awkward silence, Amanda managed to get her voice under control. "Thanks for the warning, Millicent. I know you risked a lot to do this."

Millicent tossed her head with some of her old arrogance, "Hey, I don't want your blood on my hands."

CHAPTER TWO

Exhibitors at the World Championship Horse Show in Montreal, Canada came from most of the countries of the world. Many knew about the white stallion that was burning up the show ring in the States. When Amanda or Garth neared Tornado's stall, they usually found a knot of people gathered, looking in at their horse.

"I say, Sir, when does he make an appearance?" a British gentleman asked.

"Open Jumper tonight," Garth answered.

"By Jove, I don't intend to miss it."

"Is true, Senor, he never be loser?" The question came from one of the Argentineans.

"Never even close." Jim couldn't resist bragging a little.

" 'Ow big is he then, Matey?" an Australian asked.

"Eighteen Two."

"Biggest thoroughbred I ever saw."

Two elegant young men from the Italian group sauntered toward Amanda. They wore dove grey jackets, casually tossed over their shoulders and walked with a swagger. They smiled warmly at Amanda, "Buon giorno, Signorina." Their white teeth flashed in their tan faces. The taller of the two stepped back, looking Amanda up and down, a slow smile teasing the corners of his mouth, while the second man pointed to Tornado and asked, "He's a jump this night?"

"Yes," Amanda said in a high voice that surprised her. Her cheeks felt hot.

A few feet away, Garth walked out of the tack room door and stopped. Two strangers were standing close to Amanda looking down at her in a way that made his neck prickle. Lengthening his stride, he tried to act nonchalant when he walked up to the group and put his arm around Amanda's shoulders.

"Issa boyfriend?"

"Yes," Garth said quickly. Neither Italian took his gaze from Amanda. Tornado stretched his long neck over the stall door and pushed the manicured hand that rested against his stall. He almost knocked the Italian off his feet. A smile pulled at Garth's lips, but he bit it off and pretended concern that the man's flawless jacket might be stained.

When they left, Amanda turned to Garth, "Did you put Tornado up to that?"

"Why shucks, Ma'am, you know I wouldn't do a thing like that."

Tornado bobbed his head and nickered.

* * *

At 9:30 pm the Open Jumper class began. The ring blazed with light and the smell of freshly raked tanbark hung heavy in the air. An announcer's voice quieted the crowd, "Ladies and Gentlemen, it's now time for an event that has caused much interest this evening, the Open Jumper class." There was a shuffling of feet and clearing of throats.

Tornado had drawn the next to last position and, as the event proceeded, the difficulty of the course became apparent. Two of the horses stumbled, the first negotiating a sharp turn and the second over a six foot fence. There were no perfect performances. The gate swung open and Tornado's white body trotted into the ring with Garth in the saddle. The young man's red hunt coat outlined his straight back and broad shoulders. Tornado began to soar around the course.

"My God, he's magnificent," a spectator whispered, "but he's too big to make some of these tight turns."

Tornado came to the zig-zag and jumped in, spun so sharply he looked like he was hinged in the middle and soared over the angled jump. The close set triple in and out fences he leaped like a deer, soaring into the air, landing, setting his feet and taking off over the next jump; hitting the ground and sailing over the third obstacle. He and Garth might have been cantering through the fields of home.

When the stallion rocketed over the final fence, a thunderous ovation took Garth by surprise. The entire crowd was on its feet and pulsated with the roar of clapping hands. Garth grinned, unbuckled his hunt cap and saluted the audience. He cantered out of the arena, leaned down to scoop Amanda up in his right arm and set her in front of him. Tornado arched his neck and tossed his head. The three of them paraded back to the barn with cheers echoing in their ears.

* * *

The next morning the two young people sat on a bale of hay outside Tornado's stall. Amanda leaned back against the barn, laughing. A few feet away Kathy chatted with two men, trying to answer questions about Tornado, and Jim leaned against the wall with his arms crossed, talking to a member of the show committee.

"Kathy," he called, "could I interrupt you for a moment? There's something this gentleman would like to discuss with the four of us." Kathy excused herself, looking relieved to be finished with the difficult German accents. Amanda and Garth stood up, brushed the hay from their jeans and joined the group.

The official began, "As I just told Mr. McKenzie, your horse has caused quite a stir. He's all anyone seems to be talking about. Have you ever tested his limits?"

"What do you have in mind?" Jim asked.

"The show committee met this morning and we, also, spent time talking about your Tornado. It was suggested that tonight, after the intermission, we take a few minutes for your stallion to put on a solo performance. Perhaps extending the jumps, starting at about six feet and raising them until he reaches his limit."

Jim shook his head. "We'd never ask that of Tornado. He'd kill himself for us."

The Montreal official pursed his lips for a moment. "Would you be willing to put on any sort of exhibition?"

"Tell you what, we're on our way to breakfast," Jim said. "Let us talk it over and we'll get back to you."

* * *

When they'd settled into a booth, Amanda's father started the discussion, "OK, let's hear it. What do you think?"

"I'm not sure I see any point," Kathy began. "What possible difference could it make?"

"I don't think we've even started to find out what Tornado can do, Mom." Amanda's eyes were shining, "He loves to jump. I'll bet he'd have fun."

"I think Amanda's right. He was just getting started last night," Garth said. "What if we set a height limit?"

Amanda's mother turned to her husband. "What do you think?"

"I've gotta admit I'm curious to know if he can clear eight feet. I think the world's record is eight feet one something."

"Let's set the upper limit at eight two. I think Tornado can do it, especially if Amanda rides." Garth looked over and grinned at her. "Carrying her weight must feel like no one's up there."

Jim turned to Kathy. "Are we for trying it?" Three heads nodded.

* * *

The spectators hurried back to their seats after intermission. Excitement crackled in the air. A single six and a half foot post and rail jump loomed on the tanbark. When the crowd was seated, the gate opened and Tornado walked into the ring. The spotlight shone on him and he glistened like silver. Amanda looked small on the enormous horse.

"Ladies and gentlemen, we come to the moment we've been waiting for. Tonight marks the first time we've showcased an animal in our arena. The stallion, Tornado, from the McKenzie Stables of Kentucky, US, will attempt to break the official world record high jump, which is eight foot one and one-quarter inches. You're watching history in the making, folks."

The grandstand hushed.

"We begin with a six foot six inch fence and will increase the height by six inches after each successful effort. The final attempt will be an eight foot two inch hurdle. Tornado is ridden this evening by one of his owners, Miss Amanda McKenzie. Miss McKenzie, if you please."

Amanda adjusted her hands on the reins and leaned forward. Tornado moved to his right and cantered in an arc toward the jump. He floated over the barrier to a round of polite applause. Two blue-coated ring attendants ran out and raised the obstacle to seven feet.

"Miss McKenzie." The polished voice again invited Amanda to repeat her round. Horse and rider flew over the fence with ease.

"Thank you, Miss McKenzie. Gentlemen, if you please." The blue coats dashed into the arena and raised the jump once more.

"Tornado and Miss McKenzie will now attempt to clear a seven foot six inch hurdle." People sat forward in their chairs, watching intently. Few people had ever seen a horse jump a seven and a half foot fence. The only sounds were the hoof beats of the stallion. He gathered himself before the jump and vaulted into the air, rising above the top railing, seeming to hang for a moment before dropping down to the tanbark arena. The audience gasped.

"Now, Ladies and Gentlemen, we come to the supreme test of this animal. Stewards, the jump please." The jump rails were now so far above the ring steward's heads they were using poles to put them in place. A group of officials in black tuxedos marched to the center of the arena and made a great display of measuring the accuracy of the height from the top pole to the ground.

"This is it." The announcer's voice almost broke. He cleared his throat and went on, "This stallion, Tornado, will attempt to clear an eight foot two inch jump, breaking the official world record."

Tornado's hoof beats could be heard again. The muscles in his shoulders surged with power as he galloped toward the jump. He reached the massive wall of rails and took wing. Amanda lay low on his neck, with her hands stretched down, allowing him his full head. His body arched high above the top railing. He swished his tail in the air, rocked his hindquarters over and dropped to earth. Two or three inches were visible between his hoofs and the top rail.

The grandstand erupted. When the gate closed behind the girl and the stallion, they were mobbed. Amanda could see Garth and her parents trying to reach her, but Tornado was completely surrounded by smiling faces and reaching hands. Flash bulbs blinded her, shouting voices deafened her. Fifteen minutes later they made it to Tornado's stall where an even larger crush of people waited.

It was after midnight when the crowds thinned and the four happy owners clustered around their horse and hugged him and one another. Amanda drew a deep breath, "Ummm, smell those burgers. I'm starving."

"Come on, let's celebrate. I'll even spring for a side of fries." Garth grabbed her around the waist and they headed for the burger stand. They were leaning against the building, waiting for their order, when a ring steward hurried toward them. "You have an urgent phone call," he told them.

* * *

Garth sat down at the show steward's desk and picked up the phone. "This is Garth Bannock." He glanced up at Amanda, put his palm over the receiver and mouthed, "It's Millicent." He listened again, and then answered, "Yeah, Tornado broke the world record tonight."

Amanda heard the buzz of Millicent's voice coming over the phone.

Garth answered, "I'm not sure where we're going next. We were going on to the Winnipeg show but this may change things."

Millicent spoke again.

"What?" Garth asked. "I can't hear you very well." He waited for her response. "Do you think it's that bad?"

Amanda could hear Millicent's voice rising.

"Okay. We'll talk to the folks and we'll be careful. Thanks again, Millicent."

When Garth hung up, Amanda said, "That sounded bad. Very bad. Is she still scared for us?"

"Real scared. There was a lot of static on the line, but she overheard something about us and she thinks we are about to be eliminated."

* * *

Amanda, Garth, Jim and Kathy sat up talking until past three in the morning. The young people hadn't told their folks how much danger they were in. Millicent might just be over dramatizing, as usual. They said it was Tornado someone was out to get.

"I was going to cancel the Winnipeg show," Jim said. "It's so darned far away and there's not much point competing in another jumper class after tonight, but I got a call from the Winnipeg show officials. They're all excited about Tornado coming to their city. Put a big spread in the local papers and they're getting up some fancy 'whoop-de-do' for us. I sorta promised we'd be there."

"I guess it doesn't matter where we go," Amanda said. "We can be chased anywhere."

The group decided to go on to Winnipeg, but to take a different route. Instead of traveling along the north shore of Lake Superior, they would take Route 11, which was longer but looked safer. Kathy and Jim planned to travel ahead to inspect the stables in the towns where they would stay. They would also hire a private guard to watch Tornado every night.

It was late afternoon of the following day when those plans changed.

CHAPTER THREE

At dusk the green and white horse van marked McKenzie Stables started across a causeway spanning one of Ontario's small lakes. Garth was at the wheel and Amanda sat in the passenger seat leaning over an atlas, tracing the red line with her finger. She heard Garth growl something under his breath, then the girl's right side was thrown against the passenger door as a grey semi truck crashed into their van, slamming it into the guard rail. The truck ricocheted off. The truck driver cranked the wheel hard right and rammed them again. Their van nearly overturned and wove violently from side to side while Garth fought the wheel, tires squealing. The big rig came back to finish the job. It sledge-hammered them with such force, the van pitched over the railing and plunged into the water.

"Open your window and swim under the bridge," Garth shouted. "Stay out of sight. I'll get Tornado."

Amanda struggled with the door handle, pushing against yellow-green water which gushed into her face through the open window, slowly filling the cab. With her mouth pressed against the ceiling, she pulled in a long breath and wiggled through the opening. She swam underwater through the pea soup toward a dark shadow to her left. Her lungs ached when she finally burst to the surface, gasping. Above her the causeway loomed. She swam to a piling and wrapped her arms around the rough wood. Her feet touched an apron of concrete beneath the piling and she found a foothold and clung to the support, shivering.

Above her car doors slammed and excited voices shouted. Amanda's heart began to pound. Where were Garth and Tornado? Surely they couldn't hold their breath much longer. A blond head popped up in front of her, and then Tornado's massive body surfaced. The horse clambered up onto the concrete and Garth grabbed the other side of the piling, breathing heavily. The voices from above grew loud and shrill. Feet pounded along the pavement.

"Has anyone seen a phone?"

"Yeah, 'bout half a mile back."

"I didn't see anyone come to the surface. They must be trapped inside."

"Poor devils. What a way to die."

Garth moved closer to Amanda and spoke into her ear. "We'll stay under the bridge until it's darker, and swim to shore."

Tornado stood quietly and the three waited. Soon they heard the wail of an aid car and the higher pitched scream of a police unit. A boat holding rubber-suited divers sped across the water, sweeping the surface with beams of light. The trio under the bridge kept their heads low, breathing the sharp smell of creosote and listening to the conversations above them.

"Did anyone see what happened?"

"I seen the whole thing, officer. A big truck just kept a bangin' on this green van. I think they had a horse in back – of the van, not the truck. Anyways, he hit 'em three, maybe four times and finally knocked 'em right through the rail and inta the water. I never seen nothin' like it. The creep never even stopped."

"We saw it too, officer. My husband and I were right behind this gentleman and we both saw a truck hit the van and keep hitting it until it drove it over the railing. No one could have gotten out."

"Did you get a good look at the truck?"

"It happened so fast…"

Amanda and Garth listened to the conversation overhead as darkness closed in around them. Garth wiped water from his face, leaned over and whispered, "I don't think we should let anyone know we're alive – even the cops."

Amanda nodded. When their bobbing knapsacks drifted past, Garth snagged them and nudged Amanda, pointing to the faraway shore.

The three began swimming west, staying under the roadway and stopping for breath at every pontoon. The voices on the bridge slowly faded and each time they looked back, the pool of lights grew smaller. They could see tiny figures of divers plunging over the side of the police boat.

An hour later they dragged themselves ashore and dropped to the grass. Tornado walked onto the beach, shook himself and lowered his muzzle to check Amanda, then Garth. He stood quietly waiting for a signal. The red and blue lights still flashed far off in the distance and the boat's searchlight glimmered on the water. Everything was silent around them.

They rested for a few minutes. Garth nudged Amanda and gestured with his head toward the prairie. Amanda got up on stiff legs. They picked up their sodden bags, threw them over the horse and Garth leaped astride, pulling Amanda up behind him.

They rode the rest of the night. When first morning light crept into the sky, they found a dense grove of pines. Amanda jumped down and spread her arms wide, "I can't believe we're alive."

"I think we did it." Garth hopped down beside her. "No one saw us."

CHAPTER FOUR

Laurence Duke picked up his phone on the second ring.
"We got 'em, boss."
"Tell me."
"We shoved 'em through the rail and into the drink. No one got out. Both kids and the horse went down."
"How do you know? They can swim."
"Da place was swarmin' with cops. Even a boat load of divers came and searched. There's too much deep mud here and the whole shebang sank like a rock."
"Good work. Are you sure no one can identify you?"
"Der was no name or nuttin' on the truck we used. We took the plates off. No way anyone can find us. Anyways, it probably looks like an accident. Hit and run at most."

Laurence Duke put the receiver in the cradle and a slow smile spread across his face.

* * *

Kathy looked at her watch for the twentieth time in as many minutes, then went to the window, pulled a corner of the curtain back and looked into the parking lot. "I'm getting concerned, Jim. They should have called us. They know where we're staying."

"I'll check with the Mounties, if that'll make you feel better." He dug out the phone book and began pawing through it while Kathy continued to stare into the driveway. "Hello, my name is James McKenzie. We're expecting a green horse van and it was due some time ago." There was a long silence. Kathy turned from the window and looked at him with raised eyebrows. Jim's face was as pale as death.

* * *

Amanda opened the soaked packs, sorted through their belongings and hung their clothes on bushes to dry. They also found soap and toothbrushes, packs of jerky, a couple of candy bars and some fruit. There was money in their wallets. They wouldn't starve.

"Last night while we were driving, I saw the lights of a town. I'm going to walk back and buy some stuff we'll need. Don't let anyone see you while I'm gone."

Amanda put her hand on Garth's arm. "We've got to phone our parents. They need to know we're not dead."

"I know." He stared into the distance. "I wish I knew how to tell them. What if their phones are bugged? If only I'd had some proof to show Sheriff Clark when I went to him."

"Is there any way to get hold of him now?" Amanda asked.

"What if there's a tap on his phone, too? We've gotta keep these crooks from the syndicate believing we're dead."

Amanda nodded.

After Garth left with a knit cap pulled over his hair, Amanda took Tornado down to a stream running through the trees and led him into the water. She began rubbing his satiny coat with mud. He swung his neck around and watched.

"Not much like I usually treat you, is it?" She worked a long time covering his huge frame with the slimy goo, then stepped back to check her work. "Good, you look terrible. I can't even hug you." She sat down on the grass and leaned against a pine, thinking of her parents.

A twig snapped nearby and she jumped up and ducked behind a rock. Tornado stood quietly looking to the left as Garth crouched through the underbrush and whispered, "Amanda?"

She sprang out, letting her breath out.

"I brought you each a present." He pulled a bag of jelly beans out of the brown paper sack. Amanda laughed; Garth loved jelly beans. "And for Tornado." He flourished a bunch of carrots. "Next, I've got good news and bad news. Which first?"

"The good."

"We're on the front pages of the two papers I saw. We've been given up for dead."

Amanda shivered. "Gives me goose bumps."

"They think we were trapped in the cab of the van—been dragging the lake but there's deep silt. It'll probably never be found."

"Let's have the bad news."

"If they do find the van and we're not in it, it might dawn on someone that we got away."

"Well, I'm not going to worry about that now."

Garth pointed to the stallion, "Hey, Tornado looks great."

"What are we going to do to disguise ourselves?"

Garth pulled a blue and yellow box from the paper sack. "I got some black hair dye for me." He looked at Amanda. "You can be my kid brother. I figure you can wear this cap and stuff your hair up in it. Anyway, I don't think there are many people around here to see us."

He laid out the rest of the things he'd bought; dehydrated food, a big, fierce looking knife in a sheath, a map of Ontario, a compass and two blankets.

Amanda picked up the dye and began to read, "Let's see what the directions say for making your hair black. This should be fun."

When she finished the job, she had a hard time keeping her face straight. Garth had bought a rinse, not a dye and his hair had turned greenish brown.

"It says this'll wash out after a while, it's not permanent." She looked up from reading the back of the box, "I don't know what I'd call your hair now. Khaki green, I guess." The corners of her mouth twitched.

"I'm glad I didn't buy a mirror." He looked at her. "Now me proud beauty," he said, twirling an imaginary moustache, "to turn you into a boy. This isn't going to be easy." He walked slowly around her grinning. "You take a fella's mind off what he's 'sposed to be thinking about. Here, try this big shirt of mine."

She put it on and tucked her hair into the cap.

"Well, I guess that'll do." He ran his fingers through his olive hair. "Amanda, if we meet anyone, try not to look straight at them. Keep your eyes down. No guy ever had eyes like yours."

She walked across the small clearing, modeling her new look.

"Gosh, I forgot about the way you walk."

"What's wrong with the way I walk?"

"Nothing, absolutely nothing. But there's plenty wrong with it for a guy."

"Gee, if I can't look at anyone and I can't walk, people will think I'm weird."

"Maybe that's what I'll tell 'em. A little off in the head." He was shaking with laughter.

"You're just getting even 'cause I made your hair green."

CHAPTER FIVE

Amanda and Garth had been riding for hours, when they saw the smoke of a campfire. As they neared, Garth slipped from the horse's back, held his finger to his lips and left Amanda and Tornado in a small clearing while he crept forward. He heard the low growl of voices. Three men slouched around the fire passing a bottle of whiskey. Garth watched for a minute, then turned to sneak away.

Two rough hands grabbed him from behind, nearly jerking his arms from their sockets. His back crashed against a huge tamarack tree. Two brawny men held him in a vise-like grip. "Sneakin' roun' spyin', er ya? What might ya be up to, boy?"

Garth struggled for breath.

"Wager he's not alone. Take a look, Joe." One of the beefy figures lumbered off, carrying a rifle.

Amanda and Tornado waited in the clearing. The horse snorted and raised his head, ears back. Amanda turned and saw the glint of the setting sun on the barrel of a rifle. She flinched at the sound of a click as the man cocked it.

No Tornado! The girl spoke to her stallion through their extrasensory language. *He'll kill you,* she silently warned. The horse lowered his head and quieted, but he never took his eyes from the stranger.

"I'll be damned. A kid and a horse." The man wore a greasy bandanna tied around his head and had a bushy red beard. He nudged Amanda with the barrel of the gun. "You two git in front a' me an' just walk nice an' slow."

The three of them walked toward the camp. Amanda kept her eyes lowered and tried to plod along in what she thought looked like a boy's walk. When they trailed into camp, she saw Garth with his arms tied behind him, roped around a tree. Her captor gave her a push and she stumbled into the center of the opening, falling at the feet of two menacing strangers.

Garth pulled against the ropes binding his wrists. "Leave him alone. He's my brother and he's not right in the head."

The men weren't paying much attention to Amanda, anyway. The powerful horse looked like a trophy worth having. He was the largest horse they'd ever seen and he seemed strong.

Be gentle and tame. They'll kill you if you give them any trouble, Amanda signaled.

The three inspected their prize and opened the packs on his back. "Ain't much in here but junk." They led Tornado away from the camp and chained him to the sturdiest tree they could find. They returned to the campfire and passed the bottle around, congratulating themselves on their stroke of luck.

"Dat's da biggest damn horse I ever seen."

"Seems gentle."

"What're we gonna do wid da guy and kid?"

"Don't matter. Leave 'em tied. If dey ever git loose, we'll be long gone wid da hoss. Kid's stupid, he ain't no trouble."

Time passed and they broke out a new bottle. Garth worked at his ropes. His wrists throbbed, but he continued to twist the cords. The men's voices grew louder and their speech began to slur.

Amanda watched and waited. When she thought they were pretty drunk, she began to crawl toward Garth. She had covered most of the ground, when a filthy hand closed over her face and lifted her into the air, driving her head backward into a tree trunk. Garth heard the whack of her head against the wood.

"You pig," he snarled, rage sweeping over him. He tried to tear his wrists through the ropes, throwing his body against the tree with all his strength. He whistled for Tornado and heard the stallion's chains rattle as the powerful animal lunged against them.

Amanda slid slowly down the length of the trunk, crumpling on the ground. As she slumped against the rough bark, her knit cap caught and pulled from her head. Cascades of dark hair fell around her shoulders. The man bent over and touched it. He grunted, dropped to his knees and tore at her bulky shirt, ripping it open. "It's a woman!" he yelled.

For the first time in his life, Garth knew the taste of terror.

The other two stumbled over to stare down at her. "That's a piece a work," one whistled.

"You touch her and I'll kill you." Bile welled up in Garth's throat and nearly choked him. He could smell the hot, sour stench of their lust.

"Ha. Lover boy wanna keep thish lil' dolly all fer hisself, eh? Who's first?" One of the men laughed and staggered up with a bucket of water, dumping it over Amanda's face. Garth could hear her cough and gasp.

"Garth." Her voice was barely a whisper. Garth struggled to stand and lunged with all his strength, trying to tear the tree up by its roots.

A rope loosened.

* * *

Amanda felt water splash in her face and opened her eyes. She saw three faces leering down at her. Or were there six? They kept spinning around one another and circling. They looked like balloons painted with ghoulish grins, whirling and whirling. Nothing would stand still. "Garth," she tried to speak but wasn't sure she made any sound. Tornado, I need you.

She heard chains clanging, then the sound of hoof beats. She caught sight of Garth. He swung a rifle butt at one of the balloons and it vanished. Tornado came charging with his neck thrust out, teeth bared and ears plastered to his head. He looked like a demon from hell and another balloon vanished.

She turned toward the tree and crawled hand-over-hand up the trunk. The world tilted sideways and she had to stop to hang on for a moment. She'd almost made it to her feet when she heard hoof beats again, felt a strong arm encircle her and swing her up onto the horse

The world spiraled around her head and she lay back against Garth's shoulder. He held her so tightly she could hardly breathe and he was shaking. "Is it cold?" she thought. "Why is he shaking?"

On and on they galloped. "How can Tornado see when it is so dark? Are his hoofs touching the ground? I can't hear any sound." She laid her head back again, felt the cool wind on her face and closed her eyes.

* * *

When Tornado finally slowed and came to a stop, Garth had no idea how long they'd been flying over the land or where they were. He lowered Amanda to the grass and covered her with his coat. He tasted dried salt on his cheeks. He put his head on his knees and tried to stop thinking about what might have happened. Tornado came nearer and touched Garth's hair with his nose. The horse lowered his head and dropped to the ground, lying beside him. Garth felt the comfort of the big, warm body and gradually the shaking subsided. He rested his head on the horse's neck and eventually fell asleep.

The next morning the sun shone warm when Garth opened his eyes. For a moment he was disoriented, and then the memories flooded back. He sat up and looked at Amanda lying on her side near him. There was clotted blood in her hair. He touched her cheek with his fingertips and she turned onto her back and opened her eyes.

"Ooh, that hurts." She struggled to sit up. "What's happened to my head?" She put her hand to the back of her hair, feeling the lump and clotted blood.

"Do you remember anything about last night?" Garth asked.

"I remember balloons with awful faces smiling at

me. I tried to call to you, but couldn't make any sound." She closed her eyes for a moment, "I sent a message to Tornado and you two came and made the balloons disappear. That doesn't make any sense, does it?"

"Probably makes more sense than you think."

"I remember you were tied to a tree and I tried to get over to untie you. What happened to my head?"

"There were three men and one of them threw you against a tree."

She sat quietly for a while, frowning with the effort to think, "Did they find out I was a girl?"

"Yeah, they sure did."

"Did I walk wrong? Is that why?"

Garth threw his head back and burst out laughing. He laughed harder than he had for days and felt some of the torment drain away. He remembered the comic way she'd clumped into camp last night.

Amanda looked at him and started to laugh, too.

Garth tried to catch his breath, "You've no idea what we're laughing at, do you?"

Amanda tried to shake her head, wincing.

He started to laugh again and reached out to pull a piece of grass from her hair.

In the morning, they continued heading north into the vast unpopulated stretches of Ontario.

CHAPTER SIX

Garth sat cross-legged in the grass, studying a map. He'd been quiet since they made camp and Amanda didn't interrupt his thoughts. Tornado spent the late afternoon grazing, but finally raised his head to watch his silent friends. He shook his thick mane, blew through his nostrils and walked over to Garth. He lowered his muzzle and pushed the map.

"Wanna' play, huh?" Garth jumped to his feet. "OK, big shot, you asked for it." He ran past the huge horse, giving him a whack on the rump as he sped by. Tornado whirled and gave chase. Amanda joined in and the three of them began their own version of tag, leaping from behind trees, shouting and laughing until first Garth, then Amanda, fell panting to the ground. Tornado stood before them, front legs set wide apart, head lowered, waiting for more.

"We give up," Garth gasped. Tornado whinnied and stamped his hoof.

Amanda got up and staggered over to him in an exaggerated pretense of exhaustion, "Have mercy, Great White Stallion. We're only poor humans."

The animal snorted and tossed his head.

"What a horse," Garth said. "Carries us all day and we can't tire him out at night."

Amanda bent and picked up the map. "Do you have any idea where we are?"

Garth shook his head. "I guess the next settlement we see, I'd better go in and try to find out."

"Which direction did Tornado go the night we escaped from those men?"

"I haven't a clue. Wasn't paying much attention." Garth turned to her, "I've been thinking, if those gorillas can read a newspaper, they might put two and two together and figure out who we are."

"Let's hope they're as dumb as they look."

* * *

The next morning Amanda spotted what looked like a small town off to the east. Garth set out on foot and almost missed it. There wasn't much to find: a general store, a saloon, a gas pump and a cluster of small, wooden houses in need of paint. Half a dozen dogs lounging in the dust got to their feet and set up a discordant barking when he walked down the only street.

A hand-painted wooden sign told him he was in Silver Saddle. A rusted newsstand leaned against the front of the store. If he was right about the date, the papers were two days old, but he took one, put it under his arm and went in. The plank floor was neatly swept. The building smelled of a mixture of fresh bread, stale tobacco smoke, old wood and new varnish. It took a minute for his eyes to adjust to the darkness.

"Hi, son. What can I do for you?" The deep voice sounded friendly.

Garth squinted and made out a figure behind the cash register. "I just need a coupla' things." He dug into his front pocket, pulled out a crumpled list and smoothed it on the counter.

"Don't see many strangers in these parts. What brings you to Silver Saddle?"

"Just wandering the territory. I don't like crowds."

"You sure come to the right place." While he talked, the man in the white apron pulled items from the shelves and assembled them on the counter.

"Is this the most recent paper?" Garth asked.

"Most recent one here. The papers come by mail twice a week. Tomorrow there should be another one."

"This'll do. What do I owe you?" He dug again in his jeans and plunked the money on the counter.

"Thanks, stranger. By the way, there's been a couple of grizzly sightings around these parts. Better keep your eyes open. They're mean sons a' guns."

Garth gathered his purchases and left. The dogs began barking again and two dirty children stopped playing to watch him as he tried to slow his feet and stroll up the street. A yellow dog followed him until he whirled and aimed a handful of gravel at it. He checked his compass and broke into a trot. He spotted the tall pine tree he'd marked and burst into the clearing.

The white stallion dozed with his eyes half closed and Amanda sat beside him, humming to herself and weaving a crown of lavender wildflowers. She looked up. "That was quick."

He fell on one knee in front of her, throwing his arms wide. "I can't stand to be away from you." She gave him a push and he sprawled backward laughing. "Actually I came back to see how hard you work while I'm gone," he said, pointing to the flowers.

She stuck out her tongue and plopped the flowers on her head. "Did you find out where we are?"

He reached for the map, "I don't know if that little town'll be here." He began running his finger down the index.

"What's it called?"

"Silver Saddle."

Amanda moved beside him and several minutes passed as they both searched the map. "Here it is way over here," Amanda said.

Garth leaned toward her and followed her finger. "How could we be so far from where we started?"

"The night we ran away from those men – I couldn't hear Tornado's hoofs hit the ground. It felt like he was flying, but I decided I must be dreaming."

Garth gazed at her for several seconds, and then turned to look at the horse. "Tornado's not like any horse I've ever seen or heard of. He does things there's no way to explain."

She stared into the distance and nodded.

* * *

Despite her fear, Amanda would never forget these days in Canada. Most mornings she and Garth ate a large breakfast. Bushes abounded, thick with fat, purple berries. They found a walnut tree and stuffed their packs with nuts. Amanda even stumbled upon a bird's nest and helped herself to eggs.

Tornado and Garth hunted together, the stallion circling far out in the meadows, slowly weaving back and forth, driving small game toward the man. Amanda often stopped what she was doing and stood watching. The stallion worked like a prize cutting horse, planting his rear quarters and jumping from left to right with his front legs, cutting the game off wherever it darted while herding it into range. The young man learned to use his knife with deadly accuracy and usually bagged a grouse or quail for dinner.

* * *

One morning Garth walked along the bank of a stream swinging the trout he'd just caught. He came around a sharp bend in the river and stopped in mid-stride. Thirty feet in front of him Amanda stood in the water with her back toward him, bathing. Her dark hair hung in a long sweep between her shoulder blades, a trickle of water running down her spine. He saw the slender curve of her waist, her rounded hips and thighs. His breath caught in his throat. His pulse pounded. "I'm not going to make it," he mumbled. He turned away and threw himself into the cold water.

That afternoon Amanda felt Garth's eyes following her every move and gesture. It made her feel flushed and ill at ease. At last she turned to him, "Garth, is something wrong?"

He took a deep breath, "Yeah, I guess there is." He walked to her and put his hands on her shoulders, "Amanda, I've run out of will power." He touched her hair. "You're the most beautiful woman I've ever seen, and I don't want to do anything to hurt you."

"You could never hurt me."

"I can't be with you like this and not have you. I love you so much."

She stepped closer and wrapped her arms around his neck.

CHAPTER SEVEN

Three mountain men had been drinking for several hours and grew louder with each round. They stood by themselves at the far end of the bar. Their stench was too much for most of the crowd, even though there weren't many freshly washed bodies in the room.

A Royal Canadian Mounted Policeman rested his elbow at the other end of the bar, sipping a coke and keeping his eye on the Saturday night crowd. An old piano tinkled in the corner, glasses clinked across the stained mahogany, chairs scraped and feet shuffled. The noise level climbed and the Mountie grimaced and glanced at his watch. Just then he caught a snatch of conversation.

"Biggest damned horse I ever seed."

The lawman leaned forward and squinted down the bar.

"That devil could'a killed us."

"Da little broad was sure somethin'."

The officer moved closer.

"We shoulda plugged the guy right off."

The Mountie broke in, "You say you saw some people and a big horse?"

Three shaggy heads turned. "We don't say nothin'."

"I asked 'cause there's a reward offered for a bunch

like that," he lied. The word "reward" had the effect he hoped it would.

"How much?"

"Don't remember. Considerable, I think."

That news loosened a tongue. "A real big horse, awful dirty, but light colored."

"With a real nice little gal an' a big guy. The guy and the horse near kilt us."

"Where'd you see them? Around here?"

"I dunno where in hell we was."

The Mountie moved between the men. "Looks like you might be about to earn yourselves some money."

* * *

Garth strolled down the main street of Heatherton. He felt more relaxed each time he went into a settlement. No one questioned him and he and Amanda and Tornado had been as alone in the woods as if they were the only beings on the planet. His hair had washed blond again and he carried the cap in his pocket instead of on his head.

He spotted the general store. At the paper rack out front he rummaged for change, plunked it into the slot, opened the door and stopped with his hand on the paper. A photo of Amanda and him with Tornado beside them filled the top half of the front page. "ARE THEY ALIVE?" the headline asked. His hand began to shake as he grabbed the paper and turned, grocery list forgotten. Every instinct urged him to run but he kept his pace leisurely. He dug in his back pocket and fished out the cap, pulled it over his hair and walked as slowly as he could manage with his head down.

When he was out of sight he began to run. He ran all the way back to camp and collapsed, breathing hard, pointing to the headline. Amanda picked up the paper, gasped and sank down beside him to read.

Three woodsmen had seen a big horse traveling with a tall young man and a girl dressed like a boy. The men couldn't positively identify the people and weren't sure of the location. After the story appeared in earlier papers, a shopkeeper from Silver Saddle phoned the authorities to say a young fellow resembling the picture in the paper had been buying supplies. "Even had a scar on his cheek," the storekeeper said. "I warned him about a grizzly and he left in a hurry. I wondered at the time if he had someone stashed in the woods." The article ended with a plea for anyone having additional information about these three to report to the Royal Canadian Mounted Police.

Amanda handed the paper to Garth and sat on the ground with her knees drawn up, looking into space. She heard the paper rustling as Garth read. When he finished, he sighed and said, "I guess we should have known we couldn't go on like this forever."

"Must be awful for our parents to read this in the paper."

"I've been thinking about them. I've thought of a plan, but it's dangerous."

"Seems like everything we do is dangerous," Amanda said. "What's the plan?"

"We haven't been able to call Sheriff Ed Clark or our folks because we thought their phones might be bugged. Now I don't think we have any choice, we've gotta take a chance on the sheriff's phone. If the chance turns out wrong and his line is tapped, our call will let the thugs know for sure that we are alive and exactly where to find us."

Amanda got up and walked over to Tornado, leaning her forehead on the horse's shoulder, "We're getting in way over our heads."

"We're already in over our heads. What else can we do? Run for the rest of our lives?"

Amanda straightened and turned to Garth, "I know—you're right."

"At least the Sheriff can let our parents know we're alive."

"That's the first good news today." Amanda smiled, "I feel better already."

"There's more," Garth went on, "and it's the most dangerous part. We're gonna be the bait in a trap."

"I'm not sure I feel better anymore," she tried to joke, but her laugh sounded hollow.

"We're going to move some place the Canadian Police pick out for us. Could be a place where the crooks will think we've been hiding the whole time. When we're there, the sheriff will let it slip to the mob somehow exactly where to find us. We want the gang to think that neither the sheriff nor you and me know they found out where we are."

Amanda dropped down beside him again, watching his face.

"The Mounties will plant enough men around us to make sure we don't get hurt."

"That part sounds good."

"When the gunmen come after us, the Mounties will be waiting to nab 'em before they get anywhere near us." He slapped his hands together with a smack, "They'll spring the trap."

* * *

Weeks earlier, Kathy and Jim had pulled into their driveway, returning home from Canada without their daughter or the champion white stallion. They sat in the car for over an hour. They couldn't go in to the house that waited, empty and quiet as death. When they finally opened the front door, cold enveloped them. It smelled dank and musty and faintly of leather. On the stair landing, Kathy caught the essence of Amanda's perfume. The woman sat down on the top step and lowered her head to her hands.

The people of the valley had tried to help. Solemn neighbors carried in covered casserole dishes, cakes swirling with frosting, pies with dark berry juice staining the crust. Kathy took no interest.

Their friends wanted to help with a memorial service and worked with Jim and Garth's parents, the Bannocks, to plan it. Kathy took no interest.

Each day Fitz came to the house to report on small events at the barn. The new mare had her foal, a handsome filly; their top stud was booked solid into August; two of their yearlings brought over $11,000 at the sales. Kathy took no interest.

"I hear her at night," Jim told Doc Rutledge. "She paces Amanda's bedroom for hours. Locks the door and I hear her crying. God knows when she sleeps."

It was four-thirty in the afternoon when the phone rang. "Hello." Jim knew no one would answer if he didn't.

"Jim, it's Ed Clark. I need to speak with you and Kathy about a detail in our hunt for the kid's killers."

"Come on over, sheriff."

"I'm on my way to Springdale. I don't have much time. Can you meet me at the junction of Highway 20 and Oak Creek Road? It won't take long."

"You mean right now?"

"If you can, Jim."

"Yeah, I guess I can. I doubt Kathy will, though."

"Bring her, Jim. Bring her."

Ed Clark owned an isolated cabin a mile up Oak Creek Road; he knew it would be private. As he drove, he tried to think about how to tell the families. Greta and Phil Bannock's car pulled up a minute or two behind him and when McKenzie's arrived, the sheriff saw Kathy seated beside Jim. Ed rolled down his window and waved the cars to follow him.

The caravan turned into the cabin driveway, parked and Phil Bannock pulled his hand brake and got out, "What's going on here, Ed? You're acting mighty mysterious."

Ed unlocked the cabin door. "Come on in, folks. You're right. I brought you here under false pretenses. Sit down, everyone." He went to the front window and parted the flowered curtains and peered out. Satisfied that no one had followed, he turned to the waiting group. "This is going to be a shock to you and I don't know how to break it to you except to blurt it out. Amanda and Garth and Tornado are alive."

The room stilled. No one moved. The only sound was the occasional creaking of the cabin timbers. At last Kathy turned to Jim. "What is he saying?"

"My dear friends, I had a phone call from Garth about two hours ago. His exact words were, "Tell them we're alive and we love them.""

The Bannocks held on to one another's hands so tightly their knuckles shone white. Kathy had one hand clasped to her mouth and tears spilled down her cheeks and over her fingers. Suddenly they were all on their feet, thumping one another on the back, hugging, laughing and crying together. Ed blew his nose and wiped his eyes; this seemed to be his afternoon for doing that.

He held up his hand, "Folks, I know how many questions you must have. If you'll sit down, I'll tell you everything I know." When they quieted, he told them the entire story, ending with Garth's plan to lure the killers into the open.

"Oh no! They can't do that. I couldn't lose them again," Kathy said.

Ed explained that their children would never be able to come home as long as these men were free. Amanda and Garth would have to spend years in hiding. Any contact with their families would be impossible.

Kathy sat quietly, hands folded in her lap with her eyes down. She finally nodded.

"I'm not sure Amanda and Garth realize how big this case is," the sheriff went on. "A national gambling syndicate is after them. I've been working with the RCMP and the Ontario Provincial Police. I'm sure we can spring the trap without much danger to the kids." Ed didn't feel the confidence he hoped he projected. "For the moment, you must continue to act grief stricken. You're being watched, we're sure of that. Any change in your attitude would be confirmation that Amanda, Garth and Tornado are alive, and we don't want them to know for sure until we are ready. You'll have to be good actors. Their lives depend on it." Tension crackled in the room. "We're sure your phones are bugged, too. That's why Garth and Amanda were afraid to call any of us. You've got darned smart kids."

The group didn't break up for an hour. There would be no contact between them in the next few days. If Ed needed to reach them, they arranged a signal and a meeting place. Other than that, they would not hear from him until the trap was set and ready to spring.

CHAPTER EIGHT

Garth's hair now hung to his shoulders and had bleached straw white. It glowed against his bronzed skin and his white teeth shone when he grinned. He always carried his knife, sheathed, in his waistband and he and Tornado hunted like a precision team. They thought of it as play.

The milk-white stallion galloped far out on the grassland, head high, mane flying in the wind. He began circling and weaving, driving game toward Garth. With a soft whirr, the young man's knife flew like an arrow. It rarely missed.

Amanda delighted in watching them when they worked together. Garth's back bulged with power and his muscles looked iron hard. Tornado became a silver meteor streaking through the fields.

"I'm going to miss this," she sighed, her mind wandering back over the warm, lazy days. "It's been like a long picnic with the two I love most in the entire world." She inhaled, smelling the fresh green grass and the sharp fragrance of pine needles baking in the sun. A fat black and yellow bumble bee droned past, settling near her on a clover flower. "I've never been so happy."

* * *

At last the time came for Garth to call Sheriff Clark. Ed answered on the first ring, his voice tense. "Do you have a map, son?"

"Yep, right in front of me."

"See a little town about twenty miles northeast of you called Nettle Junction?"

"Uh…got it."

"About a half mile north of there, you'll find the ruins of an old mill. That's going to be our trap. I'm sure the floors will hold that big stallion of yours, but be careful, this is a real old building."

"What's the timing?"

"Get there as soon as you can. The police are setting up right now. Later today we'll leak your whereabouts to the mob. If all goes according to plan, we should wrap this up as soon as the killers have time to get to the mill. Maybe tomorrow."

"Let's hope all goes according to plan."

"Any questions?"

"What are we supposed to do?"

"All you need to do is be there. You're only the bait, remember that. Law enforcement will do the rest. Good luck, son, we're all praying for you."

"Thanks, Sheriff, guess we'll see you soon."

* * *

A man called Joe, wearing a shoulder holster, slouched at a paper strewn desk talking on the phone. Cigarette smoke clouded the air. He shot upright in his chair, stamping out his cigarette butt in the overflowing ash tray. He put his hand over the receiver and mouthed to a bearded man seated across the desk, "They ain't dead."

His companion pushed his black fedora hat back with his thumb and swore under his breath.

"But Boss…" Joe got no further. He held the receiver away from his ear and waited, rolling his eyes toward the ceiling. He started to speak again, and then clamped his mouth shut as the tirade on the other end of the phone continued.

"Yeah, I gotcha, Boss." He clicked the phone into its cradle and took a handkerchief out of his pocket and wiped his forehead. "Duke's sore as hell."

The bearded man got up and began to pace back and forth in front of the desk, "I still say they're dead, them and the horse. I saw 'em go over the side, Joe."

"They're alive, all right. The Boss put a tap on the phone at the girl's house. This mornin' the Sheriff called her family and spilled everything, even where the kids and horse have been hiding."

The bearded man sat down again, "What's the big deal with two kids and a horse, anyway?"

"They know stuff that could put us all in the slammer—or worse." He drummed his fingers on the desk top. "Get the gang together—every torpedo we got. We're going to Canada."

* * *

The next afternoon the young people and their stallion found the mill without any problem. Trees and vines overgrew the wooden boards, but Tornado walked straight to it. Amanda and Garth slipped from his back and pushed the door open. It creaked like the door to a long-sealed tomb. They smelled the musty odor of damp wood. Dust danced in a square of sunlight. They crept in. Garth tested the floor, moving his weight up and down. It seemed solid.

They were standing in a large room. The ceiling towered three stories above them, shadowed and dark. Shafts of light knifed through the cracks between the wallboards. Stairs with several steps missing led up to a second and then third level. Walkways ran along one side of the vaulted room like catwalks. They found two doors at the far end of the main room, pushed the left one open and looked down into water running beneath the mill. Once there must have been a floor in this room but it rotted out long ago. The second doorway led down a hall with dimly lit cubicles opening from it. The silence was deep and unbroken.

Amanda went back outside and led Tornado into the main room. She saw no sign of life. If the Mounties were here, they were well hidden.

They spent the rest of the afternoon exploring the old building. Most of the windows were broken; those that weren't were so covered with grime and cobwebs light barely came through. The wood groaned and grumbled when they walked from room to room. Cold seeped into their bones—a dank, chilling cold that made them shiver. They spent two hours behind the building gathering armfuls of grass. They didn't dare take Tornado outside for even a few minutes. In the floorless room they lowered an old bucket and pulled water up for him. They heard no one; they saw no one. That night they slept nestled up to Tornado, wrapped in each other's arms.

Wednesday dragged. Being shut in like this made them feel caged. Tornado had eaten all the grass, but they were afraid to venture outside for more and lazed on the floor, leaning against the wall. Tornado stood in front of them swishing his long, silken tail at the droning flies.

Amanda jumped when the stallion threw his head up and snorted, standing stiff legged, neck arched, staring at the doorway. The girl grabbed Garth's hand and held tight, her eyes focused on something he couldn't see. After several seconds she shook herself out of the trance and turned to Garth, looking frightened, "There's a grizzly out there."

He knew better than to doubt her, "How close?"

"It's coming this way. It's close."

Tornado stamped his hoof and shook his heavy mane. He seemed unable to stand still and paced the wooden floor, stopping to raise his head and test the air. His eyes glinted large and dark and a sliver of white flashed at the edges. He kept his body between the young people and the doorway, finally turning to face the entrance with his legs braced, head lowered and nostrils flared, prepared for battle.

* * *

The Royal Canadian Policeman named Robert hated stake outs. This one was especially rough, crouching in the brush for hours. The bugs were eating him alive and his left leg ached with a cramp. He still had an hour to go before his relief came on duty. The other officers stationed around the old mill were probably as miserable as he was. Yesterday hadn't been so bad. He'd watched a young man and woman arrive, riding an enormous white horse, seen them slip from the animal's back and enter the mill, the girl returning in a few minutes to get the horse. Later they came out and spent time tearing up armloads of grass. At least, it had been something to look at. He'd been here all day surveying a lifeless landscape.

He heard movement to his left and turned his head, catching a rank animal smell. Silently he drew his gun and remained motionless, staring into the dense foliage. Nothing moved. Birds had even stopped singing and the crickets were quiet.

Without warning the woods erupted. He heard a muffled cry to his left, then a roar that seemed to come from all around him. A gunshot cracked directly in front of him, then another. He saw a figure sneak through the front door of the mill. Before he could act, the underbrush ripped apart and a gargantuan creature rose up not ten feet from him, bellowing. He looked into its open mouth at yellowed fangs. Six inch claws extended from enormous forepaws. He fired two shots point blank, then fell to the ground, rolled into a fetal position and tried to lie dead still. The bear dropped to all fours; Robert could feel its foul breath on his neck. It grunted and swiped him with a paw and he realized his own warm blood was spilling down his back. The bear pushed him with its snout. Robert remained motionless. Finally the animal moved slowly away, toward the mill.

* * *

Joe could see the old mill through the trees. He adjusted his holster and signaled the gang to fan out and surround the old building. He crept toward the front opening and had just about made it to the door when he heard a voice cry out. He dropped to the ground. An animal roared, at that moment a gunshot, then another shot. He made it to the door, darted through and dropped to the floor, crawling inch by inch along the inside wall.

What the hell had happened? Two more shots rang out. Were the rest of the gang inside yet? He didn't dare move until he knew more.

* * *

Amanda and Garth strained to listen, trying to understand what was going on outside. Claws raked across the door in front of them, rusted nails screeched as they pulled out of the old wood and the door was torn off its hinges.

The opening filled with the silhouette of a bear. He stood on his hind legs with his forepaws resting above the doorframe. The upper part of his shoulders and head weren't visible, but they could see blood trickling down his coat. The building shook as he threw his weight against it, bellowing with pain and fury.

Amanda ran into one of the cubicles and found an iron pole. She grabbed it and dashed back into the large room, as Garth unsheathed his knife.

* * *

Tornado remained facing the doorway, head lowered. He barred his teeth and thrust his head forward. The young woman and man stood on either side of the stallion, ready to fight to the death. The horse lunged at the belly exposed in the opening. The bear screamed, dropped to all fours and raced into the building. He blinked and tried to orient himself in the sudden darkness. Tornado reared and walked forward on his hind legs, slashing with his hoofs. The bear rose up again. As the two animals came together, the floorboards began to creak and tremble.

Garth and Amanda dashed toward the rickety stairs and clambered up to the first balcony. With a thunderous crash the floor beneath the animals gave way and the bear hurtled into the river below and was gone. Tornado leaped back to solid footing.

Amanda felt Garth's body grow tense beside her. In two swift movements he crouched, then launched himself onto the back of a shadowy figure she had not seen below them. Light gleamed from the steel of the killer's gun and the girl realized it had been pointed at Tornado.

Garth and the man struggled. Garth tried to free his hand to reach his knife. Amanda ran to the stairs, jumped over a missing tread and fell through, as the rotten wood gave way. She tumbled onto the floor beneath the steps, scrambled to her feet, picked up her pole and ran toward the brawling figures. They rolled on the solid end of the floor, first Garth on top, then the stranger. When the dark head came up again, she swung her pole and crowned him. The thug fell forward and lay still.

From outside they heard a moan, then grunts of men scuffling and another rifle shot. There was no way for them to know how many were out there or who they were. They decided not to take a chance on the outcome.

Garth and Amanda vaulted onto Tornado's back and the horse turned, galloped down the hallway and the three of them sailed through the large broken window at the end of the hall.

That was when Amanda heard a volley of shots, felt Garth slump against her, and then a searing pain jolted through her body.

CHAPTER NINE

At five thirty Thursday afternoon the first RCMP 'copter flew over the old mill. When it landed officers leaped to the ground and found what looked more like a battlefield than a stake out. Robert was sitting on the ground, blood running down his back, apparently dazed and talking about a bear.

Inside the mill they found a gaping hole in the center of the floor and the rank smell of bear fouled the air. They saw a crumpled gang member in the corner, unconscious. They found four more in the woods, one with his scalp nearly torn off by the bear, another alive, but badly injured with a bullet in his chest. Two cursing gunmen were handcuffed around a tree.

The first hint at headquarters that something had gone wrong came at four thirty in the afternoon, when the transmission from the mill sputtered and broke off in mid-sentence. It took more than an hour to reestablish communication. To say the operation had not gone as planned would be an understatement. A huge grizzly had appeared on the scene and, at that point, the reports from officers grew confused. None of the troopers could explain exactly what had happened.

When they arrived, the Mounties pieced the story together. The horse and young people had been seen arriving Tuesday by law enforcement officers, and seen again later that afternoon. No one had spotted them since. None of the officers knew what had happened inside the mill or what had become of the young man and woman and their horse.

The inspector put off contacting Sheriff Ed Clark in the states. He didn't know what to tell him. How could a large horse and two people vanish without a trace from the scene of such mayhem? Were they wounded? Maybe there'd been more gang members hidden in the woods and they had taken Amanda and Garth hostage—or killed them. There were more questions than answers.

By mid morning the following day the inspector felt confident his men had captured all the gunmen at the mill. They were in custody, turning states evidence in an effort to save their own skins. They were spilling evidence and naming names from all across Canada and the US. He decided he could no longer put off the call.

The inspector reached Ed and filled him in on what he knew. The operation had gone smoothly until a grizzly upset their plans. "We've got several of these bums in jail and they're starting to sing. This is the syndicate we've been trying to nail for years. It's a big one – operates here and in the states."

"Any names?" Ed asked.

"I don't want to say too much on the phone. We're still questioning them right now."

"I think I may have the leader down here."

"Good work! Keep him under surveillance, don't let him out of your sight. We should have all you'll need to make arrests in a day or two. These kids of yours have helped us break this case wide open. They're real heroes." The inspector paused and cleared his throat, "In the meantime, finding those two and their horse is our number one priority. I'm gonna put bloodhounds on their trail."

* * *

Tornado galloped for over an hour carrying the dead weight of his friends. When he finally slowed, he was in a glen beside a stream. The late afternoon rays of sunlight cut through the trees, dappling the grass. The stallion walked to the stream bed and lowered his body beside the water. Amanda stirred. The horse shifted his body and gently slid his human burdens onto the grass.

Amanda opened her eyes and tried to focus on the branches overhead. Slowly flashes of scenes at the mill, of the bear and of their escape through a big window, came back to her. She turned her head and saw Garth lying near her, his shoulders in a pool of blood. She tried to raise her head, but felt a weakness so great she dropped back and drifted into a dream.

The night seemed endless. Amanda floated in and out of consciousness. Once she came to her senses with her face in the stream, drinking deeply. She felt on fire. She slipped away again, lost in a shadowy world of phantom visions.

Garth moaned. Tornado went to stand beside him and laid his muzzle against the young man's cheek. "What?" Garth whispered, his mind hazy with pain.

Tornado moved to Amanda's body. He began gently moving her nearer to Garth, then the horse lay down as close to the girl as he could, with his legs tucked under his upright body. He grabbed Amanda's jeans in his teeth and swung his head around, trying to pull the girl onto his back.

It was more than an hour before Garth managed to help the stallion, then to crawl onto the horse himself. At last they were both astride Tornado and he got to his feet. Amanda lay with her head on the horse's mane and the young man's body draped over her, clinging to the horse's neck. Neither of them moved.

Tornado stepped cautiously lest he unseat his precious cargo, gradually gliding into a long striding canter. The riders began to stir. The horse galloped faster and faster. The trees whipped past at breathtaking speed and gradually dropped away beneath his hoofs, fading out below them.

Garth lifted his head first and shook the hair from his eyes; Amanda slowly sat up with an expression of wonder on her face. The young people felt as though they were astride a streaking comet and looked back, seeing the shimmering blue ball of earth slowly shrinking, while the frozen orb of the moon loomed before them.

Tornado galloped on. His hoofs met the marble surface of the cratered moon and pounded so the beat pulsated through their bodies. Clouds of moon dust encircled them. Amanda's long, dark hair whipped in the wind and Tornado's silver mane streamed across their bodies and his tail swept behind them like a meteor trail. They laughed to the music of his hoof beats.

Tornado whinnied and threw his head in the air and launched into the ocean of space. The threesome was transported through the stars. They watched a spray of diamond crystals wash across their path, joined the Milky Way and melted into its crystalline rivers. Their faces glowed with rapture, their laughter echoed through endless galaxies.

On and on they galloped.

* * *

Bloodhounds bayed, hot on the trail of their quarry. They had the scent of the stallion and easily tracked him through the woods. At last they came to a sun dappled clearing beside a stream. The grass was bloody and matted with hoof prints leading to and from the stream. The hounds began to circle, the scents of the horse and his human cargo strong in their nostrils. They plunged into the stream and crossed it, scouring the grass on the opposite side with their noses. Up and down the shore they searched, plunging from side to side in the water, unable to pick up any scent of the horse leaving the clearing. At last they stopped and stood still, panting.

Amanda, Garth and Tornado had vanished as though they had been snatched from the surface of the earth.

CHAPTER TEN

A factory worker named Jeff ended his shift at midnight and stopped in at Clancy's for a beer. One mug turned into two before he pushed away from the bar.

The fresh air felt good on his face. The moon looked like an enormous pearl shimmering down Windsor Street. It reminded him of a painting he'd seen somewhere. Something stood at the end of the street, glowing in the moonlight with a strange inner light. He began to walk faster. It looked like a statue. Yes, a marble statue of a big white horse towered in the middle of the plaza, bathed in moonlight. No wonder marble was the stuff of great works of art, he thought. It looked luminous.

He crept closer, scarcely daring to breathe. The statue moved. Jeff's eyes grew wide and his heart began to hammer. He whirled and ran to the corner, turned right and sprinted up the steps of the Provincial Police station. Ned was the constable on duty. Jeff burst through the door and almost fell as he tripped over the threshold. "There's a big, shining horse standin' 'round the corner," he shouted.

"What in thunder you been drinking?"

"I'm not drunk, Ned. I tell ya, I seen it with my own eyes. Looked like a statue at first, but then it moved."

"Hold on a minute, I'll lock up and we'll check it out."

When they opened the door, the first thing they heard was hoof-beats echoing through the deserted streets. The constable jogged down the steps and walked to the corner with Jeff tiptoeing behind him. He peered to the right and saw an immense horse walking away from them. It looked as if there was something on its back. The two men turned the corner and followed.

* * *

Peggy's day started at two a.m. when she unlocked the bakery and started the bread dough and cinnamon rolls. She loved the walk to work when the moon was full and there was no one around. She felt alone in her own enchanted world. This night the silence was broken by a faint sound. It reminded her of hoof beats and it was coming nearer. She ran to the corner and turned. The biggest horse she's ever seen was walking toward her. As he passed, she saw someone slumped over the animal's neck, arms hanging down.

She held out her hand and spoke to the horse, but he walked on. She was wrong, there were two people on its back. They both looked dead. Constable Ned Bainbridge and Jeff Simpson trailed behind and Peggy fell in beside them. "What's going on? Are those people alive?"

"Don't know, Peggy. Jeff spotted them a while ago. I can't get near the horse. He acts like he knows where he's going."

By the time Tornado walked up to the entrance to the hospital, there was a small group following him. The Constable went into the lobby and hollered, "Anybody here?"

A woman in a white coat came around the desk. "What's all the commotion?"

"We've got a big horse out here with two people on his back. Don't know whether they're dead or alive. We haven't been able to get near enough to find out."

The doctor rang and two orderlies appeared. Now that Tornado had reached the hospital, he allowed people to approach him. The orderlies carefully lifted Garth down.

"Get a couple of stretchers. This guy's still alive."

They reached up and pulled Amanda's limp body to the ground, laying her gently on the stretcher. "She's got a pulse, but it's awful faint."

"I'll bet I know who these people are," said the Constable. "Remember the young man and woman and horse—a big white one I'm almost sure—who were in all the papers a while back? They were being chased by a bunch of gangsters and there was a showdown at an old mill up north. Cops captured the whole gang, but the horse and kids vanished. There's been a real manhunt going on for them." The article was coming back to Ned. "Seems the horse is some kind of champion. They're from the States."

The hospital personnel carried the stretchers inside and the townspeople stood around talking for a while, then slowly broke up and drifted off. By morning the story had spread all over town.

The constable went back to the station and rummaged through his files, finally coming up with Sheriff Ed Clark's name and phone number. He glanced at his watch. No point in calling until later. Maybe he'd know more.

Before he went off duty, he called the hospital. The young man had a fifty-fifty chance, but things looked bad for the girl. He picked up the phone and dialed Sheriff Clark.

CHAPTER ELEVEN

Garth opened his eyes, blinked at pale green ceiling tiles and smelled disinfectant. The last thing he remembered was a fight at the mill. After that a strange, delirious dream in which he and Amanda rode Tornado across the surface of the moon and over a pathway of stars. His heart began to pound as the memories came into focus. It seemed so real. Could it only have been his delirium? He closed his eyes.

When he opened them again, someone was taking his pulse. "Good evening, Mr. Bannock. How nice to have you back with us. How're you feeling this evening?" A nurse with red hair and a snub nose stood beside the bed holding his wrist. He tried to answer, but nothing came out. "Just a minute," the nurse went on, "there's someone here who'll be glad to see you."

He smiled. It must be Amanda. A hand touched his forehead and he opened his eyes again. His mother and father sat beside the bed. "Hi, son. How're you feeling?"

"Okay I guess. Where are we? How did you get here?"

"We're in a hospital in Canada. We've been here a couple of days, praying for you to come out of a coma." His dad leaned closer. "You've been hurt real bad, but it looks like you have turned the corner."

"Where's Amanda?"

"She's right in the next bed, by the window."

He turned his head. She was sleeping. "Is she all right?"

"She's still in a coma."

* * *

During the next two days Garth was able to spend some time out of bed. Amanda still lay quietly, hooked up to bottles and monitors.

Garth was in the adjoining bathroom when two doctors came into the room. He overheard one say, "There's nothing more we can do. She may not last the day."

Garth burst into the room, "Get Tornado. Bring him to the window."

The doctors stared at him blankly, "You mean the horse?" one ventured.

"Get him now!"

They stood staring at the young man.

"Hurry! Bring him to the lawn outside her window."

The doctors left the room quickly and stopped in the hall, looking at one another, "I've heard some goofy requests when a loved one is dying, but this is a first. What do you think? Should we do it?"

"The poor guy's been through a heck of a lot. Where is the horse, anyway?"

"Her family'll know. They're in the waiting room."

Kathy and Jim looked up when the doctor came into the room and told them what Garth had asked. Jim pulled on his jacket and headed for the stable. He could hear Tornado trumpeting a block before he reached the barn. He found the horse pacing the stall, covered in sweat with white foam flecking his shoulders.

"We ain't been able to do nothin' with him," the groom said. "Whinnies and carries on something fierce. Seems to be in a terrible state."

Jim tried to quiet the horse, snapped a lead rope to his halter and opened the door. The stallion charged out, almost knocking Amanda's father off his feet. The big horse pulled the lead rope through Jim's hands and galloped straight to the hospital, the sound of his hoof beats ringing through the streets. He cantered across the lawn to the window of Amanda's room and thrust his head through the open window, touching her hand with his nose.

Garth went to the stallion, put his arm around Tornado's neck and spoke to him for a few minutes. The horse tossed his head and snorted, then lowered his head toward Amanda's arm, his lips brushing gently across her hand. Garth moved to the other side of the bed. Leaning over the girl, he rested his left forearm beside her head and began to speak in a low voice, "Amanda, I'm here and so is Tornado. We won't let you slip away from us. We're waiting for you in the meadow." Garth's deep voice continued to speak to the failing girl.

Most of the hospital staff had heard about the strange request and from time to time they found a reason to look in on the scene in Room 104. A nurse asked the doctor on duty, "Is there a chance?"

The doctor shook his head. "Doubtful."

The story began to spread through the small town. People walked or drove past the hospital to see the towering stallion standing at the window. By dinner time, there was not a household in town that did not know of the lonely vigil the horse and young man kept at the bedside of their loved one. The phones at the hospital switchboard rang constantly. Each caller received the same message. It seemed hopeless. A pall fell over the community as they waited for the drama to play out to its tragic conclusion.

"We won't let you go, Amanda. You can't leave us." For hours the only sound in the hushed room was the low murmur of Garth's voice and the soft sounds made by the horse.

Amanda's lips trembled.

Garth reached under her shoulders with his left arm and gathered her closer, "I'm holding you, Amanda. Tornado and I are here waiting for you. Here's my hand. Reach out and take my hand, Amanda."

The fingers on the girl's right hand quivered.

"She moved her hand. I saw her fingers move," a young nurse ran down the hall, calling to the intern. The head nurse and the intern returned with her to the open door. The scene looked as it had since early morning. The intern stole in to look more closely and shook his head.

"They twitch sometimes in comas. It doesn't mean anything. I think we should try to stop this guy, though. He's going to kill himself. How long has he been there?"

"All day. He was there when I came on duty and so was the horse."

"Come on, Mr. Bannock, it's time to rest." The intern took Garth's shoulders and tried to turn him away.

Garth didn't react. He didn't seem to know there was anyone else in the room.

The head nurse wiped her eyes. "There's something beyond our understanding happening in there. Everyone who sees them feels it."

"Lost," Amanda whispered, so faintly the nurse and intern didn't hear.

Time ticked away without another sign of life from the girl. The young man and horse never stopped calling to her.

"Cold," her lips hardly moved, but Garth and Tornado heard.

"It's warm here, my love. Tornado and I are waiting for you in the sunlight."

Amanda's eyelids fluttered.

"You're almost with us. We can see you walking down the path to us." He took both her hands in his. "I'm pulling you closer. Do you hear Tornado?"

The horse became agitated and his murmurings grew louder.

More people gathered in the doorway.

Amanda opened her eyes.

"Garth? Tornado?" she whispered. "I couldn't find you. It was so beautiful in the stars. I didn't want to leave, but I got lost."

The horse let out a piercing whinny that echoed through the hospital corridors. Garth buried his head beside hers and sobbed.

"Is she gone?" an orderly asked.

"No, look, her hand is moving."

Her fingers moved through Garth's hair. Her other hand rested on the nose of the stallion who had stood outside her window all day and half the night.

THE END

EPILOG

Amanda's mother sat at the big, round kitchen table. Greta, Garth's mother, sat across from her, cradling a coffee cup in her hands. "With Laurence Duke in prison and Buddy in a mental institution, what's to become of Millicent?" she asked.

"She's still living in the big house." Kathy slowly stirred her coffee. "Her old governess moved back to be with her and there's still a staff of servants."

"Kind of a lonely life."

"She may be better off than with that father of hers." Kathy looked up and smiled. "Anyway, Buddy's much better. He should be home with her soon." Kathy leaned to the end of the table and pulled a pile of papers toward them. "Maybe we'd better get to work on these. Look at this stack of proposals. These are offers from film companies. These are from book publishers, and this bunch over here are requests for product endorsements."

Greta shook her head, "Have Garth or Amanda looked at any of them?"

"They don't even seem to care."

"Our children have changed, Kathy."

Kathy looked up from the papers, "You've noticed it too?"

"They've grown up, but it's more than that. Garth has a tie with Amanda that shuts out the rest of the world. Tornado's part of it, too."

"Amanda insists the stallion is never to be locked in a stall. There's some deep bond that joins all three of them."

"I guess we'll never know what happened during those weeks in Canada—we'll probably never understand."

Kathy sighed. "I've watched the three of them walk out into the pasture together, lost in some world of their own. When I look again, they've vanished.

CPSIA information can be obtained
at www.ICGtesting.com
Printed in the USA
FSOW01n1256180515
7119FS